IN THE LAND OF LIGHT

BOOK 1

THE PROTECTORS,

IN THE LAND OF LIGHT

L.D. Warken

WRITERS REPUBLIC L.L.C.
515 Summit Ave. Unit R1
Union City, NJ 07087, USA

Website: *www.writersrepublic.com*
Hotline: *1-877-656-6838*
Email: *info@writersrepublic.com*

Ordering Information:
Quantity sales. Special discounts are available on quantity purchases by corporations, associations, and others. For details, contact the publisher at the address above.

Library of Congress Control Number: 2021930381
ISBN-13: 978-1-63728-015-7 [Paperback Edition]
978-1-63728-108-6 [Hardback Edition]
978-1-63728-016-4 [Digital Edition]

Rev. date: 03/01/2021

CONTENTS

Prologue		xi
Chapter 1	Why Are My Fingers Tingling?	1
Chapter 2	Screaming and Gasping and Retching. Oh, my!	11
Chapter 3	My Sulking Gets Disturbed	20
Chapter 4	The Ally	28
Chapter 5	The Principal's Office	33
Chapter 6	Why: My New Favorite Word	39
Chapter 7	Bubbles Aren't the Best Weapons	49
Chapter 8	The Destiny of Muriel Wiley	54
Chapter 9	A Player Going in Blind	57
Chapter 10	A Ticket Out of Crazy Town, Please	65
Chapter 11	The Shadows Say Hello	78
Chapter 12	The Guardians	84
Chapter 13	Hearthstone	88
Chapter 14	The Addition to the Hallawells	95
Chapter 15	The Coffin Train of Doom	107
Chapter 16	Welcome to Ravenscroft	118
Chapter 17	Floating on a Shimmering Sea	128
Chapter 18	Hey, Trouble	139
Chapter 19	The Role of a Protector	147
Chapter 20	It's Hard to Say No.	153
Chapter 21	The Danger Zone	157
Chapter 22	Stones and Shadows	164

Chapter 23	Hang in There, Muriel	169
Chapter 24	Rage, Red, Wish I was Dead	173
Chapter 25	A Shadowy Past	183
Chapter 26	Watch your back, El	187
Chapter 27	Crowns, Lies, and Secrets on the Rise	192
Chapter 28	The Origin	198
Chapter 29	Invisible Hands, An Unprotected Land	202
Chapter 30	The Hope Stone	210
Chapter 31	I'll Come Back, I Promise	214
Chapter 32	What's a Squidark?	219
Chapter 33	Shadow Island	224
Chapter 34	A Snake Knocker	227
Chapter 35	We've Lost our Minds	231
Chapter 36	The Dream and the Kiss	237
Chapter 37	The Black Spires	246
Chapter 38	Just Trust, El	251
Chapter 39	Hello, Muriel	259
Acknowledgements		260
Chase		264

GRAM! I owe this one to you. You spent endless hours with me planning and editing. You are my inspiration and I can't wait to see where we go!!

With exuberant amounts of love, Lil.

PROLOGUE

Vials rattle on their shelves, some of them dropping to the concrete floor and shattering. There is another noise, like metal snapping and twigs cracking. My head whips up and I spot a dark-haired boy standing in the doorway, roots surrounding him. The door, broken off its hinges. His bright blue eyes go wide as they meet mine.

A crack begins to run along the floor. Chase and I jump back from it as it spreads. He grabs for my hand but misses as I tip backwards when the floor gives a violent shake. Crashing to the ground, my body jarrs from the impact.

The windows shatter, and the glass crashes to the floor, creating a sound like thunder. I cover my head, and feel tiny pricks of glass dig into my skin.

I spot Ri under the shattered windows, her hands over her head. Her mouth is open in a silent scream.

"Ri!" I scream, extending my hand towards her.

Ri cries for me but her shriek is cut short. She's gone. Literally. She's disappeared.

I turn back to yell at the Plant Boy but he's gone too. The only trace that he was ever there are the roots and the broken door.

"Chase, what's happening?" I pick myself off the floor in a last effort to get to him.

I run towards Chase, but slip on the chemicals that have spilled all over the floor. I fall again. The green chemicals burn my fingers.

I reach for Chase, trying to find something to steady me. He tries to grab my hand, terror written all over his face, but something whips him away.

I'm left alone in the chaos.

What is happening? Where did they all go?

I lie in a pool of green chemicals, feeling the acid as it burns into my skin, bracing for whatever is going to happen next. Glass shatters. I feel shards prick my hands as I shield my face. Shelves fall.

The ground rumbles more violently. I close my eyes, gritting my teeth. And then everything disappears in a flash of light.

CHAPTER 1

WHY ARE MY FINGERS TINGLING?

"Fight! Fight! Fight!!"

The words pound in my ears. I duck to dodge a punch, but I have never been good at fighting. The punch lands on my jaw, and I see stars. The world tips. I rub my jaw, fighting back tears. I glance up and find Al, a sneering, adolescent boy standing over me.

"How you feelin', *Smell*?" Al snickers and kicks me in the stomach. I land in the dirt, the marketplace tents coming in and out of view.

"Absolutely brilliant. Thanks for asking."

I grit my teeth, tasting blood. What was Rolia going to say when she noticed the brand-new bruises that never seemed to go away? The group of teenagers clumped around me call for blood. How did the world become like this?

"They all want to see you bleed, you disease," Al whispers in my ear, his breath hot.

I should run. I'm fast. I could get away. If only this place wasn't so crowded.

"Then let them," I say, meeting his cold eyes.

He scowls, wishing I would fight more.

"As you wish," he says, standing up, readying his fist to draw the blood the jeering crowd wants to see.

But a voice cuts in. My salvation.

"Al Buckley, you leave my best friend alone, *right now*!"

A petite blonde girl shoves her way through the circle. She places her hands on her slim hips, lips pursed. I've never been happier to see someone. You may be asking why this petite girl has a say? Because a pretty face can sway anyone. At least here, on the dirty streets of Ractia.

"We were just having some fun, Ri," Al whines, pouting. Ri scowls.

"If you don't leave my best friend alone, I'll personally pound you." To Al's credit, he doesn't laugh. Instead he raises his hands, in surrender.

"I still don't know why someone like you hangs around with her."

He jerks his finger at me. I scowl at his back and stand up, my body aching. If only I could fight, but I just get ground into the dust again and again.

"Muriel Wiley is one hundred times better than all of you combined. Now shove off!" Ri glares at every single one of our peers 'til they're all gone. She rushes over to me, her face in a worried pinch.

"El, you can't let them run you over like that," she says, taking my shoulders in her soft hands.

"I'm sorry. I just… don't know how to stop it from happening." I hang my head, and she pushes dark strands of hair out of my eyes.

"Chin up, Muriel Wiley, for goodness sake." I lift my chin and give her a crooked grin.

"Thanks, Ri," I say, shaking off her hands.

"Oh…!" Ri starts to exclaim, but she's interrupted.

"Ri Olivia Simons! What have I told you about talking with that street rat?" A piercing voice cuts off whatever Ri is going to say. Ri rolls her large, grey eyes and faces her mother, a woman with a dagger-like glare and an even nastier smile.

"Get over here, right now." How my amazing, kind friend ended up with that witch, I have no idea. Ri sighs loudly, but doesn't argue.

She starts to walk away but whispers over her shoulder with a small grin, "I'll see you at school tomorrow."

I nod and watch her retreating form, her black and white clothes much more pristine than the shops and booths around us. I glance down at my dark shirt and pants. They're mostly brown now. I release a breath, trying to beat off some of the dirt, but it sticks. Shrugging, I make my way through the market, grabbing an apple here, a biscuit there.

I don't classify myself as a thief, just a lucky passerby that stumbles upon food every so often. And the food here is much better than the rations that my robotic mom and I receive. My backpack bounces on my back, books and pencils jostling around inside as I run.

I scoop up an apple from a vendor whose shouts of anger fuel my run. The market is easy to get lost in, which is perfect for me. Sprinting behind the vendors, a smile lights up my face.

This is the one place where I can get lost in the crowd and be myself, away from hateful looks. This is the one place where I can run and feel free. The books jostle around in my backpack while I run, the apple clenched between my teeth.

I jump onto a ladder, an old friend that takes me to the top of the grey concrete walls surrounding our city. Graffiti adorns the walls in colorful patterns. Scrambling up the rungs of the ladder, my long arms and legs come in handy.

I regain my balance and sprint across the wall, which is barely wider than my shoulders. Shouts echo behind me, but no one pursues me. Street rats running in the streets is normal for Ractia, California.

I slow to a walk and brush back stray strands of dark brown hair that have escaped my bun. Sitting down on the wall, I let my legs dangle. The apple is delicious, the flavor of fresh fruit bursting in my mouth. The fruit must come from a province where it rains every so often.

The land is grey and dead, the effect of World War III, which has left the world barren. And now here we are, struggling to regain…well, our lives. The Government doesn't leave very much room for living, though.

They tell us what to eat, when to eat, what to wear, where to work. If you weren't born into a family that was higher up in the chain of wealth, it was very likely you'd be swallowed up by the world. My robotic mother and I almost get swallowed every day.

But it doesn't matter. I will climb out of all of this someday. Somehow, I'll find my freedom.

I throw my apple core and it lands thirty feet below me on the grey grass beyond the wall. No one will notice. We dump all our trash out there anyway.

Climbing to my feet, I wave my hands to remain balanced. I walk along the wall as I have always done every day since the day I started school. Now, ten years later, I'm still walking the same grey walls.

The marketplace ends, and I spot the bus station. I jump onto a roof and then down onto the hard concrete. I roll to lessen the pain. My legs have gotten used to the shock of landing on something solid from high above.

Walking down the cracked sidewalk, I pass horrors. People left to starve because they refused to work or go to school. Their rations have been stopped, and now they're paying for it.

I pass a small child sitting on the curb. She's barely four years old. She looks so lonely.

Her eyes are filled with a hollow light, her hair a tangled mess. I stoop down beside her and pull an apple from my pocket. I put on what I hope is a bright smile.

"Here," I say, extending it to her.

Pudgy, dirty hands reach out. Her wide brown eyes shine. A smile cracks the dirt in her cheeks. I rub a thumb along her face.

"I'm sorry."

I stand and walk away. I can't do anything. I wish I could take her into my arms and sweep her away to somewhere green and safe.

The only ways to get around the city are either by walking or riding the public buses. Waiting for the bus, I tap my Ear Rings, and tell Rolia that I am on my way home. The silver bus slides into view on its magnetic tracks, and I climb aboard.

I sit on the bench, leaning my head against the metal back of the bus. It sways gently beneath me. Since it doesn't have any wheels, the wind always shakes it a little. Magnets keep it hovering in midair.

The bus comes to a halt at my stop. I grab my backpack and get up to stand, but someone sticks their foot out. I tumble to the ground, books spilling everywhere.

A laugh echoes above me. Gathering my books, I slip my hands through my backpack straps, slinging it onto my back. My cheeks are burning.

"See you tomorrow, Smell," a boy, the one who tripped me, says, laughing.

I give him a nasty glare, realizing he's a kid from my school. He isn't worth my time. My real name is Muriel, but El is what I prefer to be called. Those who don't like me, which is almost everyone, call me Smell.

I hop off the hovering silver autobus and wave to the driver, who waves back. He's a rare one who shows me an inkling of kindness that none of my peers do.

After placing my hand on the lock sensor, I push open the gate that leads to my house and slam the door. My home is silver, like every other home on the street. The houses are the same color—a dull grey asphalt—with the same technology. Our governor won't have it any other way in 2421.

"Rolia, I'm home!" I call through the house, slipping into the kitchen. I lay out my day's spoils. A couple of apples and some oil for Rolia's squeaky wheels.

Rolia found me on the street when I was a child. She asked if she could keep me as her own. Surprisingly, the governor said yes.

But when I grew older, she confessed the real reason for adopting me. I was an experiment child—a way to see if abandoned children could be raised by robots. Apparently, they can, but that doesn't mean people won't hate you for being different.

But we can't do anything about it, and I've kind of gotten used to it by now, since it has been happening since the seventh grade. Being teased about having a robot mom has become normal for me.

It's not as bad as it sounds. I got teased before for my good grades and robot mom, but not like this. This is something...different.

Entering my room, I hang my backpack on the hooks that line the wall and carefully place my homework on my desk to be completed later.

Stacks of books line the rooms. A small window lets a dim light filter in. My thin blanket is crooked on my bed. I lay my backpack down, quickly slipping off my shoes, which I place in the Drepsler, an automatic cleaning machine.

I snap off the lights in my room as I traipse back outside to get some fresh air. Though I know that the air isn't that fresh. I sit on my front porch, leaning my head against the cool metal post. The sky above broods with a storm, which will soon break over the barren Earth.

Suddenly, my eyes catch something silver hovering over me. I cock my head, regarding its presence. It tilts too, coming closer from the place that it is hovering in the sky. It whistles, like wind is sifting through some sort of fan, but I can't find anything on it that is keeping it aloft.

It's about the size of my palm, with a golden star encrusted in its center.

It continues to hover, two golden lights flashing.

At first, I think nothing of it, since it must be something the Government sent out to take some sort of strange test on the human race. But the longer it comtemplates me, the more uneasy I feel. Why isn't it just scanning me and leaving?

"Target confirmed. Muriel Grace Wiley."

A high pitched whistle cuts through the air like a siren. I jump to my feet, scrambling backwards.

I don't move fast enough.

A needle imbeds itself in my thigh, as long as my pinkie. I cry out in pain, trying to grab it. My leg is slick with blood, and the needle is covered in a green slime.

Grabbing a stone from the ground, I look towards the sky, trying to locate the hovering silver orb of doom.

It's gone. Disappeared into the grey sky from which it came.

I drop the stone and return my attention to the needle. The bleeding has stopped, mostly, but what worries me is whatever was on the needle. Who knows what it will do to me.

Using my shirt, I successfully manage to rip the needle out. Not without considerable pain. My eyes water and hands shake.

Knowing the needle, and whatever was coating it, has already done what it came to do, my mind can't help but wander to the worst outcomes. The green slime, is now in my bloodstream. Whatever is going to happen to me next is unknown. But I know it won't end well.

I toss the needle to the ground and stomp on it, just for good measure.

Limping into my house, I head straight for the bathroom, hoping to get there without Rolia spotting me.

She must be busy elsewhere because I make it to the bathroom without disruption. Grabbing a rag, I wet it down and begin wiping away the blood around the wound. I wash my hands, watching the green stuff wash down the drain.

A strange sensation comes over me. My head spins, my hands shake and begin to… tingle?

I notice the toilets water beginning to boil, the faucet on the sink shakes. Backing away slowly, I raise my hands, begging the sink and toilet not to explode.

As soon as I raise my hands the sink explodes, recreating a geyser that would rival the geysers that once lay to the North. I shield my face, not daring to watch as my bathroom explodes.

The water hits the ceiling, and comes toward me like it's raining. But the water stops right above my hands.

Almost as if...

I cut the thought off before I can finish it. There's no possible way this could be happening.

If I drop my hands, the water will just keep hovering above me. Gravity or something must be off. That's what's going on here.

I drop my hands and the water splashes to the ground, soaking me.

Clenching my fists and stare at the puddles around my feet. My shocked, horrified reflection shines back at me.

I controlled the water. With my hands. The needle, whatever it was, had triggered something. Something inside of me. Something in my genes.

I flip my palms up, watching the puddle on the floor begin to rise.

The world tips, and the last thought I have before I slip away is, *This is not a normal Thursday.*

CHAPTER 2

SCREAMING AND GASPING AND RETCHING. OH, MY!

My eyes flit open. I lie on my bathroom floor, not remembering how I got here, or why I am soaking wet. My head spins, eyes hardly focusing on my surroundings. Spots of dizziness dance before my vision.

I'm lying in a puddle of water and blood. I push myself into a sitting position, and a wave of nausea hits me. I clutch the sink, attempting to pull myself to my feet. It takes several attempts to stand up, but eventually I manage to get to my feet, relying heavily on the sink.

My clothes are soaked through, and there's a hole in my pant leg.

I stare at the faucet. Or atleast where the faucet used to be. Suddenly, it all rushes back. The small silver square, the needle, my bathroom exploding, and the water listening to my hands.

A dizzy spell hits me again. I squeeze my eyes shut, too terrified of my current situation to want to try to figure out what to do next. But I will move on. That's what I always do.

I look into the mirror and find that my eyebrow is split open and scabbed over. When I fainted I must have hit my head on the sink. If the wound is scabbed over I must have been down for a while.

Why hasn't Rolia come looking for me?

I grab the rag that I had been working on my leg with and wet it in the shower and begin to wipe away the blood on my leg and face. Next, I wipe up the puddles on the floor with a towel and deposit it in the wastebasket.

Rolia can never know about the exploded bathroom predicament. If she ever found out I would be grounded for life, not to mention I would be outed to the government and thrown in jail for the rest of eternity.

The last thing to deal with is the faucet, which is still lying on the ground dejectedly. I scoop it up and stick it in the hole where it used to be. Turning the switch, water pours calmly from the opening. I'm sure this fix won't last long, but I may not even be here when Rolia discovers it.

Terror courses through me thinking of what could happen if I was ever discovered. Until I learn to control whatever has happened to me, hiding it will be impossible. I made my bathroom explode. How am I supposed to drink a glass of water?

One step at a time.

I slip calmly out of the bathroom and into my room. Grabbing a new pair of pants and shirt, I put them on quickly. I pull a cap on to cover up the cut on my head. I know I won't be able to hide it forever, but maybe till it's less pronounced.

Stepping back outside, I pick up the needle from the concrete and discard it in the dumpster that sits right outside of our home. Removing evidence is my first step to secrecy.

I sit on the porch, trying to sort through all of my thoughts when Rolia rolls onto the concrete pad beside me.

"There you are! I've been looking for you. I heard some crashes earlier, but I expected it was you falling off your bed."

I have been known for being clumsy, so I roll with it. "Yeah, whoops." I force a grin, hoping it doesn't look too fake.

If robots could give weird looks, Rolia would have given me one.

"Okay," she says. "Time to start on dinner."

I follow her into the house, telling myself to act natural, everything will work out.

But honestly, when does anything work out.

The knife hacks along the cutting board as I chop up the potatoes issued for our dinner rations. Every night I prepare dinner, while Rolia catches me up on her day.

She drones on and on about the freak explosions and never actually does any work. Honestly, she is a terrible house droid, but a wonderful mother. Somehow she's nurturing with her metal-pronged hands, wide blue eyes and almost compassionate facial expression. But her cleaning defects normally mean I get stuck with all the work.

Rolia came from a factory where they manufactured robots that served all kinds of purposes. She'd been one of the best. But a deadly gas leaked in her building, killing the robotic programmers and ruining Rolia's programming so that she was unable to perform more advanced tasks. She was turned away to the streets, along with thousands of other house robots. That's when she found me and took me in, once the Government had approved her request. And now I am hers.

I am pulled back into the present when I notice something black on the underside of my wrist.

I turn my wrist so that my palm is facing up, and almost drop the knife on my toes. Rolia goes silent, noticing it at the same time I do. There's a tattoo on the underside of my right wrist.

Could this day get any worse?

"What is that, El?" Rolia asks, her white body scooching closer to me.

"Nothing, Rolia." I pause, turning my wrist away. I add, just to make sure, "And don't tell anyone about this."

"Yes, El."

The weird thing about having a robot for a mom is that I can give her orders. It has definitely made me follow my own honor code to not lie, cheat, or take advantage of Rolia. I turn away from her and cover my mouth with my hand to stop myself from screaming, or gasping, or retching. Or all of the above, in that order.

So instead I study the markings, trying to focus on them instead of my racing thoughts. A black circle with a hand calling a blue tidal wave toward it inside the circle. The hand is covered in extravagant jewelry. It seems to be straining, as if controlling the water.

I cover it with my hand, glancing around. Body markings are not allowed. And neither is color, which means this tattoo would result in the stocks, and I can't risk that.

The stocks are in the town square. I cannot risk drawing more attention to myself, especially with this newfound thing that is happening to me. Besides, I have a mystery to solve. And so many questions to answer. Starting with: *Why is this happening to me?*

Rolia follows me into my room, chattering about some celebrity that I would care about if I was a normal teen girl. But I can't be anymore. There are more dire things at hand.

Rolia was originally programmed to be like a young girl, so she sometimes still acts like it when she isn't following the Mom Routine.

Pulling out my Flip, which is a small tablet-type device, I flop onto my bed to begin my homework.

A Flip is made from glass but has sensors inside it that enables one to do almost anything, besides the websites restricted by the Government, in the technological world. I pull it from beneath my bed and finish some homework on World War III.

I try to keep the images of twisted bodies out of my mind—the bodies of those who had been poisoned by the deadly NTO3 gas.

Instead, I focus on getting prepared for school tomorrow. I pick out my outfit, choosing a long-sleeved sweatshirt to cover the mysterious tattoo on my wrist.

We are ordered in our community to wear only the colors white and black. A part of keeping our society clean and uniformed, fitting its needs. Having no color also helps conserve resources, which is the only thing the Government seems to want to do. The Government turns a blind eye to the people who are starving on the streets and the heaping mountains of waste piling ever higher outside our city walls.

"Are you all right, Muriel? My sensors are picking up on fluctuating blood pressure," Rolia says, rolling towards me on her white tracks, her oval eyes narrowing.

"I'm all right, Rolia," I lie, fiddling with the edge of my blanket.

Rolia is someone who has always cared about me, and lying to her doesn't make me happy. But this is not something I can share. I try to put away thoughts of what has happened to me, but it is pretty much impossible. The fact that water just shot up and I controlled it, echoes around my head. Rolia is no doubt picking up on my wacky nerves.

The chime of the dinner bells, which are set up throughout the city, echo through my room. Everything is scheduled and controlled. Hasn't the Government heard that rules without respect inspire rebellion?

The bland potatoes stick to my tongue and the strips of meat barely make it down my throat. It is hard to eat when everything tastes the same. The questions bouncing around my head and the fear squeezing my stomach make it even harder to swallow.

"What story would you like to hear tonight?" Rolia asks, scooching back and forth on her tracks in anticipation. This is a routine we follow and I always ask for the same one. Mainly because it's Rolia's favorite.

"Can you tell the story of how you found me?" I ask, setting down my spoon. She won't take anything but my complete attention.

"You know it," she says with a wink. Sometimes I think she's actually malfunctioning when she does human actions. But I'll never know. I place my head in my hands, elbows on the cold steel table, as Rolia begins, reciting from the script she's written in her head.

"It was a dark and cold night. Thunder clapped and rain slashed. I rolled through the streets, looking for stray bits of oil that I could take for myself. I was almost out—the factory had abandoned me a month before. Things were looking desperate."

I nod vigorously, like I have no idea what's coming next. "Suddenly, a small cry reaches my sensors and heat waves come off from a side street." I drop my jaw to add effect.

"I roll forward, unsure of what I am to find. A small basket containing a golden blanket and…" She somehow makes her face into a visage of excitement.

"What is it? *What*?" I ask, scooching forward in my seat.

"A small baby, wide green eyes full of tears, pretty little lips trembling. Her face pale and soft around her freckles, dark hair soaking wet."

"How flattering," I deadpan. Rolia ignores me.

"I gather the small child into my arms and take her to the Government building two blocks away, begging to be able to take care of her, doubting that they would say yes. But they did. They gave you to me, along with a house and a small fund before I could get back on 'my tracks.'" She laughs, her robotic voice toning down the tinkle.

"And then I fell in love with that baby and raised her. And now she sits before me today, beautiful and kind." I blush and shove the last potato into my mouth. I go to the sink and wash my plate, stacking it neatly next to my cup and spoon, our only utensils in the house.

"That's a great story, Rolia," I say as I leave the kitchen. I pause in the doorway, and clear my throat.

"Thank you, by the way."

"For what?" Rolia asks innocently.

My heart squeezes in my chest. "For raising me, taking care of me. It probably wasn't easy."

"It wasn't, but I'd do it again in a heartbeat if it came to that."

Blinking away tears, I spin on my heels and hug her tightly. "Thank you."

I pull away and straighten my shirt, unsure of where that sudden burst of emotion came from.

Rolia prepares tea as I run through my nightly routine. She follows me into my room. The cold floor stings my bare feet. I keep rubbing my tattoo, thinking about how my day had taken a surprising turn.

Rolia follows me into my room, ready for our nightly routine of drinking tea and talking about books. It is one thing that keeps me sane.

"How are you feeling, El?" she asks as I slump onto my bed, grabbing my Flip.

"Good, as always." Grinning at her, I pull the pillows closer to me.

I fall back on my pillows and sigh, tracing my tattoo. It's a sign that there could be an escape. It makes me feel like there is something more. Which there obviously is. I mean, the proof is on my wrist. There's something out there besides Ractia, California, dirty streets, clogged market places, and black and white clothes.

But I don't know how to find it yet. Or how drastically everything could change if I did escape.

"El? You are doing that thing when you stare into space." Rolia rolls forward and pokes my shoulder with a pronged hand. I jump and blink.

"Sorry," I mumble. "It's just been a long day."

"Is there any way I can assist you?" I shake my head and take my cup of tea off the platter she's holding.

"We are on page 545, El," Rolia says, and the book we're reading, "*Future's Time*," pops up on my Flip. Since Rolia controls all the technology in the house, it doesn't surprise me. It also appears in the middle of her upside-down-egg-shaped body.

We read for at least an hour, not speaking about anything besides the book. Rolia doesn't really read, she just sits there and I narrate what's happening for her. It's our deal, since Rolia serves people around the neighborhood to buy the food on my plate and the clothes on my back. It's a small contribution for everything she does for me.

The curfew chimes ring through the room, signaling we have to turn out the lights. Just as I'm about to switch off my lights, Rolia says from the doorway, "Whatever happens, El, you just have to trust." And with that, I flick off the lights.

CHAPTER 3

MY SULKING GETS DISTURBED

Rolia comes to wake me up at the crack of dawn. I climb out of bed slowly, rubbing the sleep from my eyes. I check my wrist, unsure if the day before had just been a crazy dream. Sure enough, the tattoo is still there, a reminder that life has been turned upside down.

I should probably just run away before anything bad happens. I smile at the thought of taking off and finding my own adventure, but push that feeling down when I realize the reality of trying to escape. I'd be hunted down, then thrown into jail for the rest of my life.

I stumble over to my dresser and tug on the long, white-sleeved hoodie, black shorts, and white sneakers I had set out the day before. I put my hair into a messy bun, grab my backpack and zip into the bathroom, cursing my boring clothes. Wearing the same colors over and over becomes very aggravating.

The faucet is still operational, and intact, by some miracle. Though it isn't helping that much, because when I try to brush my teeth, I can't wet my toothbrush. The water moves away from my hand every time I attempt to wet it.

Eventually I just brush my teeth without the water and then I can't rinse my mouth. What is drinking from water fountains going to look like? The feeling from yesterday crawls under my skin. A sense of dread.

Life is going to be a nightmare from here on out. If I bend my hand the wrong way my water is going to do something weird at lunch. Then I'll *really* be hated. I'll be known as "The Freak."

Heading into the kitchen, I grab some breakfast. I order orange juice and waffles from the breakfast dispenser. Part of going to school is that the Government gives you breakfast and lunch so your family only has to take care of dinner—one more way we are forced to depend on the Government.

I lean against the counter and sip my OJ, waiting for the waffles to pop out onto my plate. My mind settles slightly as I relive what I always do in the morning, preparing my mind for the day ahead and eating breakfast, because food is always a major highlight for me.

My waffles pop out, hot and dripping in butter and syrup. My mouth waters. This is how the Government officials eat every day, fully taken care of, fat and satisfied, while the rest of us are left with their scraps.

At least I can eat like them while I am in school. Two more years after this I will have to fend for myself. The coming responsibility is daunting.

I eat my breakfast alone as Rolia busies herself with who knows what around the house. I don't have much time to eat since school starts at 8:00. Rolia comes into the kitchen and begins to count the thirty seconds till the bus arrives.

I shovel down the rest of my breakfast and sling on my backpack. I manage a weak wave at Rolia as I'm shoved out the door by her pronged hands. Mornings are always this way.

Rolia is very punctual, so I'm never late.

I punch in the code to the gate that is in the front yard then race down to the bus waiting at the small silver station. As I run the fetid stench of waste wafts up from the sidewalk and clings to my clothes. The cracked asphalt crumbles beneath my feet as I race toward the floating silver bus.

People from the surrounding neighborhoods climb on, their black and white clothes dull against the brown grass behind them. I hop in line behind people heading for work and school. The autobus takes anyone anywhere. Mainly it runs for kids going to school.

I stand in the crowd of people. Most of them have their Flips out. The screens reflect on their faces and they all appear to be a world away.

Everybody from my school is throwing nervous glances at me like they always do. Ever since the one day I screamed at our principal after he'd "accidentally" tripped Ri. No one had expected it from me, the quiet girl, who never stands up for herself when she gets told off. Or bullied. So now, everyone stares, trying to be subtle, waiting for me to lose it again.

Ri told me I looked terrifying. She said my hair started floating in the air and it seemed like I had grown taller by a foot. I had protested that maybe that's just because I was yelling so I seemed bigger. I must have been intimidating or else I wouldn't have left such a large impression. So now, I just stare at my hands, mostly used to the looks I am receiving.

I rub my wrist where the tattoo is. *I* have a secret. And a big one. One that is life changing.

World changing.

So why was this given to me?

I reach the front of the line and climb the silver extended steps. The bus just lets out a tiny hum to let me know that it is operating.

I breathe a sigh of relief as I climb onto the bus, glad to be away from the looks and glances for the fifteen-minute bus ride to my school. I shove down the aisle in the hovering silver bus and keep my eyes glued to the ground, hands on my backpack straps. I have to elbow my way to my usual seat past people going to work, school, or the market. Public transportation is always crowded.

I press back to my usual spot and plop down, not noticing that there is someone next to me till he clears his throat. I jump and whip my head around to find a blonde boy, lounging in his seat, his arm draped over the chair behind him. I move away, needing some space.

"Hey," he says, and I almost jump. No one talks here. Ever. He tugs at the sleeves of his black and white hoodie, which somehow manages to look cool with an Aztec pattern. I don't know what to say, so I don't respond.

"Sorry, didn't mean to disturb your sulking," he says with a hint of a grin on his face. There is a touch of a Southern accent in his voice, which is also strange. People rarely move anymore, since we're assigned houses and jobs. Only if you own a business, or you get offered a job by the Government somewhere else, are you allowed to move.

I raise both of my eyebrows. I'm intrigued by this boy who wants to talk. "I'm not sulking. I am just in very deep thought."

He chuckles lightly. "Sorry, again, ma'am."

I have never been called 'ma'am' before, I can't tell if I like it.

"It's okay," I say with a shy shrug. "You just surprised me."

He smiles, the corners of his sea blue eyes crinkling. His whole complexion is shining, like he got dipped in sunlight. No one is this happy around here. We all look like we got dipped in a puddle of sludge.

"All right, Ms. Moody Pants, I'm Chase." He holds out his hand and I shake it stiffly once-- not giving too much emotion.

"Muriel. But please call me El." I suddenly feel the urge to continue a conversation. It's intriguing finding someone who wants to talk instead of finding a way to pick on me. I wrack my brain for a question that won't sound trite. But that's pretty hard, since I only talk to a robot most of the time.

I feel awkward as I ask, "Are you going to school?"

"Yeah, Senior School in Midtown." I shift back fully into my seat, placing my backpack on the floor of the grimy bus carefully.

"Have you always gone and I have not noticed you?" I ask but instantly regret it when a devilish grin lights up his face.

"How could you not notice *me*?" he asks and I feel a blush rising in my cheeks. He *was* pretty noticeable.

"Um…" I say, unsure of what to do next. He just smirks, his ocean blue eyes shining, like he knew that he had gotten to me.

"We just moved from Florida." He exhales, glances away and runs a hand through his wavy blonde hair. Obviously he was unhappy about this move.

My brow knots with sympathy.

Chase shrugs, scrunching his freckled nose. "But it's okay. My dad thought Cali would be just the perfect place for his business. I'm going to miss it." A shadow passes over his eyes.

So that's what it is. His dad owns a business.

"I-I'm sorry," I murmur, twisting my fingers, not knowing what else to say. I glance out the window past him. The suburbs of Ractia flash by.

"What year are you in?" he asks.

"Tenth." I continue twisting my fingers, putting all of my stress about meeting a new person into them.

"Me too." He grins. "Maybe we'll get classes together."

"Oh, maybe." I focus on my hands, shoulders slumping. I remember what is happening to me. Having friends is going to be hard to keep this big of a secret from.

His grin falls a little.

"Come on, El, I can't be that bad." He bumps my arm playfully.

"No. You aren't." I turn away, regrouping my emotions before turning back to him.

I just then notice the headphone sticking out of his right ear. I hadn't noticed it because it had been facing the window. He twists the cord around his finger.

It's kind of strange seeing headphones with a string. *No one* uses that type anymore. There are little headphones that you can wear as earrings, or just set on your ear anywhere and it would stay. Although you can only really listen to the news or Government officiated stuff, which I normally steer clear from. Honestly, wearing headphones with strings is an act of rebellion. Listening to music is another way to show defiance. Just like how I collect paper books to protect what the world used to be.

"You could get into trouble for those," I say and point to his headphones. I would hate for him to end up in the stocks. This world needs more people like him.

He shrugs, brushing off the danger.

"Paper books are an act of rebellion too," he points out and I begin to nod in agreement.

It takes me a minute to run over his words and realize something is off. I never said anything about books. I narrow my eyes at him. And he pales. *Noticeably.* The pieces fall into place. He couldn't have just noticed it? Did I have a bookish air? Yet, I decide to go with the impossible. The last twenty-four hours proved that anything can happen.

"Chase, how did you know I read books?"

"I… made a random guess?" He glances down at his hands, which are shaking.

"Don't lie to me," I say, my voice sharper than I intend. "What really just happened?"

"Muriel… I can't just tell you."

I grab the front of his shirt, and he flinches, pain flashing in his eyes. For the first time, I'm the one calling the shots.

"Oh. I think you can." I tighten my hold, I can feel his heart beat thundering in his neck.

His shoulders are rigid. His eyes wild. Then he releases a breath and the tension that was holding him captive.

"I-I found it in your head."

I release his shirt as quickly as I had grabbed it.

Shock overtakes me. "You what?"

CHAPTER 4

THE ALLY

"Oh, you've got to be kidding me," I grumble, slinking low into my seat.

The world spins. Who else is this happening to? Should I tell him? Or leave the bus and never look back?

But he trusted you, a tiny obnoxious voice tells me. No way around it.

"I can't believe my luck," I grumble as I pull back the sleeve of my sweatshirt. The tattoo stares back at me. Chase looks between the tattoo and me, then back to the tattoo.

"Wait." He pulls back his sweatshirt and holds his wrist next to mine. It has the same circle, but inside of his, there's a brain.

"Whoa," he says, glancing at me.

Our eyes meet, and we must be having the same thought. *We both have this strange thing happening to us.* Dropping our wrists back into our laps, we sit in shocked silence for a moment.

"When… how did you get this?"

My words spill out, awkward and scattered. Putting my fingers to my head, I try to fight back the oncoming headache.

"Ye-yesterday afternoon. This needle thing attacked me while I was getting boxes from my yard. Then suddenly a killer headache. It gets worse when I touch people, though. I can't stop the thoughts from coming."

I glance at him. That's why he flinches when I grabbed the front of his shirt.

"That must really hurt. Hearing people's thoughts like that."

He nods and rubs his head.

"I'm sorry," I say, not really knowing why I'm apologizing.

He blurts out, like he has to get it off his chest, "I'm a telepath."

"*Obviously,*" I snap, a little too loudly. A couple of eyes turn our way.

I duck.

"So it happened to both of us. Around the same time…and there could be more of us."

I glance around at the other people on the transport. It could have happened to any of them.

"This is so strange," he whispers, stuffing his hands into his pockets. "We're just normal people. I have only seen movies about this kind of thing."

"We're not heroes, we're just kids," I whisper, then add, "Why would this happen to us?"

"Who knows? We're totally normal," he whispers again and crinkles his brow, like he is thinking very hard about something.

"What if my dad getting a job here was supposed to happen? What if I was mind-controlled to sit here, so that we'd meet?"

I twist my fingers, trying to make sense of all of this.

"No one could do that," I say, trying to convince myself as well as him. "It's not possible."

He nods reluctantly, like he doesn't believe me.

I glance at the tattoo that shouldn't even be there.

"Maybe you're right," I say with a long sigh. "It's just I hope that you're not."

"Me too…"

We stare at our wrists that are marked with a sign that screams that we're different, that we'll never be normal again.

I have the urge to scratch at the skin till this mark rubs away. Rubs away all of this. Wipe it from existence.

"What can you do?" he pushes, obviously trying to put the fact that he might have been mind-controlled behind him.

Except, I understand his curiosity. I have the same problem. Still, there is a lump in my throat that makes me never want to speak to Chase ever again. About any of this creepy, freaky thing that is happening.

"Manipulate water," I mumble and glance around, making sure no one is listening on the smooth-floating transport bus.

"That is *super* cool," he says. I stare at my hands, and shake my head. "I just wish none of this had happened."

"Me too, but it did, and now we have to deal with our new reality."

I nod, swallowing tears.

"How could you tell the needle affected you?"

"It stabbed my leg, and I went inside to wipe off the blood and pull my wits together. Then I exploded my bathroom." I blush, and don't look at him."

"You exploded your bathroom?" He says, in a loud whisper. "My respect for you just doubled."

"Thanks?" I twist my fingers and glance out the window, noticing we are pulling into the dingy pull in of the high school.

"Look, Chase. I imagine you're thinking along the same lines that I am. We both had this happen to us and we both don't have anyone to rely on. Unless we stick together we're alone in this. And alone will probably end in something happening to the both of us."

He nods, for once serious. "I agree. Someone to have our backs in case things go south."

"Exactly. We need to be allies, so we can survive this and figure out a plan. Because I'm sure the Government would love to kill Brain Boy and Water Girl as soon as they find out what's happening to us."

Chase pales. "You're right. Allies?" He holds up his fist for a fist bump.

"Allies." I bump his fist and sigh. "But as allies we need to have boundaries, like no mind reading, Brain Boy."

"Noted." He salutes.

I feel a grin tugging at the corners of my mouth.

"Plan number one, is sticking together. We need to get the same class schedule. Plan number two, securing our team. I have a friend who we can trust, and even if she didn't have this happen to her, we can still trust her."

"Another ally, got it."

"Okay, Mission Not Being Turned into Science Experiments here we come."

We high five and scoop up our backpacks, hopping off the bus.

We shove through the crowd with me in the lead. Ractia North High School towers over us. As ugly as always. If you were in space and you looked down you would wonder if the Earth had been covered in soot.

It's tall, black brick walls reach about two stories, and buildings are spread across the campus. No trees or plants line the concrete sidewalks that weave through the dreary school grounds. The bright California sun beats on the solar-paneled windows, creating a glare. We all meet in the main building in the morning to get stuff from our lockers.

I glance back for a moment to make sure Chase is still behind me and not lost in the crowd of rowdy Senior Schoolers. His black high tops hit the concrete right behind mine and I don't feel so alone anymore. A teammate when facing something unworldly is a valuable asset.

Now, all we have to do is survive.

CHAPTER 5

THE PRINCIPAL'S OFFICE

We head to the principal's office. Some kid bumps into my side and almost knocks me over. I stumble to catch up with my feet.

"Dude, watch it," Chase snaps, stepping in front of me, a cool protectiveness to his voice. The student frowns at him, then shuffles away. Chase glances back at me and raises an eyebrow.

"What was that about?" he asks, his voice surprisingly serious.

I shake my head.

"I can deal with them," I say quietly.

"Yeah, you handled that perfectly." He winks back at me. "No one should treat anyone that way."

"It's fine, really. Come on, Chase."

I sigh and continue on, Chase at my side, now glaring at anyone who gets too close.

My school will forever smell like B.O. and boys' lockers to me, along with other disgusting smells you don't want to know. Our mascot, a black tiger, doesn't really match the dull halls of our school. This school's mascot should be a grey sloth.

I knock on the door of the principal's office, which is a square room with pictures of our principal at award ceremonies all along the wall, along with trophies of his accomplishments.

A large bald man, pulls open the door and narrows his beady eyes at us.

"Hello, Mr. Kepler." I say, as politely as possible.

Mr. Kepler doesn't answer but motions for us to enter.

I focus my eyes somewhere above his head. I still feel his cold eyes on me.

We've never had a favorable history.

"Please take a seat, *Miss Wiley.*"

Mr. Kepler is a middle-aged man with a stern face, his cold grey eyes permanently piercing. His bald head is way too shiny to be natural. You could use it for a mirror.

I slouch down across from him in one of the plush armchairs and continue staring at his shiny head, not letting myself meet his eyes.

He is one person I am not afraid of, even though I should be.

Chase sits down too, though he doesn't slouch as much. He tries to put on a bright smile.

Mr. Kepler disregards him. Chase turns to me and raises his eyebrows in an obvious question: *What's with the death looks?*

Mr. Kepler turns slightly fidgety under my relentless gaze.

I think I terrify him, which makes me feel almost triumphant.

We have argued in the past, which has resulted in multiple demerits. I try to avoid him as much as possible.

Yet here we are.

"Who is this?" Mr. Kepler sneers in his oily voice, with a cold smile. "Didn't you read the school manual that specifies that new students should report to the check in desk. I am only here for emergencies."

"No sir, I did not read the school manual. This is a special case, this is my cousin, he's new here. I was wondering if I would be able to show him around, maybe have the same classes as him."

His bald head glistens under the fluorescent light. His temples begin to bead with sweat, his reptilian visage pinched with anger.

"Why should I help him?" he scoffs.

Chase turns fidgety.

I don't blame him.

"Because he's your student, Mr. Kepler."

I remember Mr. Kepler told us on an orientation tour before the new school year started that he doesn't care about his students. He said that he only expects the best behavior from us and not to bother him.

I wonder why he even works here.

"Do you really think that you, Miss Wiley, are the best person to assist this young man?" he snides, his beady eyes squinting.

"Yes, I think I *am* the right person for this job."

"Me too," Chase jumps in.

"So be it," he says, rather reluctantly. He turns to Chase and grumbles, "What is your name, young man?" He pulls out a registration form.

"Chase is fine, sir," Chase tells him, appearing embarrassed.

"At this prodigious institution we use formal names." He arches his eyebrows importantly. "So, your last name, please."

"Yes, sir. It's Cutler," Chase mumbles. He clearly is not proud of his last name. I wonder what secrets he is hiding up his sleeve.

"Mr. Cutler, you will join your cousin in all of her classes 'til you can manage on your own. How does this sound?"

"Good, sir. Thank you."

He shows us out, saying nothing. Now that he has dismissed us, he turns his head away, ready to be done with this conversation, and us.

"Great. Thanks, Mr. Kepler," I say dryly.

Chase smiles and shakes the principal's hand, trying to be polite. I begin to walk out of the office, slinging my backpack over one shoulder.

Just before Chase leaves the room he calls back to Mr. Kepler, "Thank you, sir, for giving me the opportunity to check my teeth before meeting new people!"

I choke on a laugh. Did he just call out Mr. Kepler on his bald head? My respect for him just bounced back a little bit.

Chase successfully closes the door before laughing.

"He's going to *hate* you forever," I say and hold my stomach through the giggles.

"Eh, it was worth it." He laughs, "I wonder how he makes it so shiny."

"Beats me," I say and shrug.

"How many new faces I'll gain today, Miss Wiley? First it was Brain Boy, now cousin. This mission is ending up with alter egos of Chase Cutler. Pretty cool, huh?"

"Oh yes, very. Come on Brain Boy, plan number two is waiting for us to carry out."

"Mission Mission Not Being Turned into Science Experiments, is fully under way!"

We head towards where I know our lockers will be, keeping my eyes glued to the floor, holding back a grin.

"Nice school," Chase remarks, his eyes trailing the white lockers and banners promoting Government-issued programs.

Senior Schoolers shuffle past, eyes on their Flips. No one is different or better. Just stuck in a world of rules and monotony.

When we get to the lockers, we find Ri, leaning against her locker, arms crossed. Her fingers are tracing the white flowers that are embroidered on her black bell-sleeved shirt that is belted over her immaculate white pants. I always feel like the trash collector when I compare my clothes to hers.

"Hey," Ri says, smiling. The smile doesn't quite reach her eyes.

"Hi," I say, and hug her quickly. How am I going to break the news to her about Chase and I? I decide to introduce Chase as my cousin, so Ri won't ask any questions."This is my cousin, Chase. We just met this morning. He moved from down South."

"I didn't know you had a cousin," she says, eyeing Chase suspiciously.

"Now I do."

"I'm Chase," he says, and shakes her hand.

"Ri Simons." She eyes him, chewing her lip. She turns to me, her eyes nervous.

"What's wrong?" I ask, fears about the needle and everything leaving my mind.

Friends are always top priority.

"I need to talk to you about something. Privately."

"Uhh…all right." I glance at Chase, and he shrugs as Ri grabs my hand and drags me to a corner.

"El, something happened yesterday that shouldn't be real."

I pale. It couldn't be. What was my luck?

"It shouldn't have been possible, but it happened somehow. And...and I couldn't call because I was afraid someone would hear it." She chews her lip.

"What is it, Ri?" I urge, taking her hand to support her. She's swaying, like she's about to faint.

"There was a needle…."

"I *knew* it," I say, not letting her finish. "Ri, it happened to me, too." I pull back my sleeve and show her the tattoo.

Ri lets loose a little sob, pulling back her sleeve.

CHAPTER 6

WHY: MY NEW FAVORITE WORD

"This is not good," I say, slipping Ri's sleeve over her tattoo. It's a circle with a snowflake inside it.

She's shaking now. "They could kill us for this," she whispers, her voice cracking.

She's always been so strong for me, but I always feel the need to protect her as well.

I wouldn't wish this on anyone.

"Hey, calm down. It's going to be okay." I soften my voice, trying to put on an air of confidence that I don't really feel. I squeeze her shoulders, attempting to give her some comfort.

Ri nods, sucking in deep breaths.

"No one's going to kill us, because no one is going to find out." I offer her a small smile.

Ri nods again, with tears glistening in her wide grey eyes.

"We are going to keep this a secret and if need be, we will leave."

Ri hiccups.

Students walk past, eyeing us.

"Y-you mean le-leaving our families?"

I nod slowly. "Please stop crying, I'm going to protect us, okay?"

"Okay, I trust you," Ri says, her breath catching as she attempts to take deep breaths.

"All right, see that boy over there?" I nod my head towards Chase, who is trying to look at us without being obvious.

"Yes," she says, eyeing Chase nervously.

"Well, he had the same thing happen to him. And we're a team now, you, him, and me. He's not my cousin, and I'm sorry for lying, but we have to be very careful." I take her hand.

"Anyone else could have had it happen to them so we have to keep our heads down. It's just going to be us three in this together."

"But how do we know we can trust him?" Ri asks, eyeing Chase.

"You trust me, right?"

"Yes, I do," she says, smiling.

"And I trust him. We're a team. I won't let anything happen to you," I reassure her again.

Ri nods. "Okay, El. I'll protect you too, we're in this together."

"We're in this together." I hug her tightly.

She glances at the other high schoolers walking up and down the hall.

She and I are probably thinking the same thing: No one can be trusted. Any of them could have the same mysterious tattoo.

"Let's go talk to Chase." I drag Ri back over to Chase.

He raises an eyebrow at Ri's puffy red eyes. "What'd you do to hurt Blondie's feelings?" he asks, patting Ri's back.

"It wasn't me, I promise. It's..." I glance at Ri and she nods, giving me permission to tell him. "Ri got the needle yesterday, too, which probably means other kids in the school got it as well," I whisper. "It's so strange how all three of us got it. Whoever is out there knew that we'd meet each other. We're being used. But any of them could be as well." I eye the crowd moving past.

For once Chase is at a loss for words. He glances at me, at Ri, and then around him.

"I take it you don't want to befriend any of them?" he asks, running a hand through his hair, making it spike in all different directions.

"No, I definitely do not. We have to keep it secret and only trust each other." I look directly at each of them, giving them my brightest smile.

Ri nods.

Chase says, "Got it."

"I'm going to get us through this," I say confidently, not knowing where this sudden boost of confidence is coming from, but knowing that I'll have to hold onto it in the coming weeks. "We're a team now."

"You've always had it in you," Ri says.

Chase gives two thumbs up.

I don't know what to say to this so I stare at my feet, uncertain of the next step.

Silence stretches between us.

How do you even begin to handle a situation like this?

"I know this sounds mental, but I kind of want to try our powers out," Chase says, so quietly I can barely make out his words.

"I was just thinking the same thing," I say. "Why not? We might as well do something with what we have." I glance at them. "We'll just have to be careful."

"Well, duh, it wouldn't be very smart to yell, 'Hey, look over here while I blast this thing apart with a tidal wave that I just summoned!'" Chase whisper-yells.

I put my head in my hands, shaking my head.

"Yes, that's true."

Chase and I both look at Ri, who is as pale as the white walls around her. She's still in a state of shock.

"Let's do it," Ri says hesitantly. "But I'm just wondering why this is happening. And to us of all people."

Chase makes an offended noise. "You don't think I'm special?" he asks with a wink.

Ri shakes her head. "Not the time."

"Maybe it is a disease?" I suggest. They raise suspicious eyebrows at me, like the implication was crazy. "Never mind...."

"Beats me," Chase replies with a lift of his shoulder.

Ri glances between us, then shakes her head.

The first warning bell rumbles through the hall. Five minutes till class starts. And we aren't any closer to knowing what's happening, but we're ready to find out.

"When should we try...whatever we are going to call this?" Ri asks, grabbing her books from her locker.

"I really don't know," I say.

"I'm new here, so I shouldn't be calling any shots," Chase says, shoving his hands into his pockets.

"After school? Or whenever we can find time that will not be obvious," Ri suggests. Chase and I glance at each other before nodding. We cannot go off disappearing during classes. That would draw attention that we don't need.

"Well then, we could use one of the labs. They're always vacant after school, and I could freeze the door shut once we got in," Ri offers.

"That sounds good to me," I say, smiling at her.

"Oooh, you have ice powers?" Chase asks. I totally forgot to ask what Ri could do. Ri nods, trying not to laugh at Chase's enthusiasm.

"What about you two?" Ri asks, leaning in with an excited smile on her face.

"I have telepathy," says Chase, "but I'm learning to control it."

Ri scrunches her nose.

"I'm sorry, that must be loud," she says, and Chase nods.

I smile at them, glad that they are coming to terms with their new reality. "I can manipulate water," I say. "And we should go. Class is starting soon." I grab my backpack, which is full of books and swing it over my shoulder.

Ri gives me a quick hug and says, "See you at lunch. I'm glad I'm not alone in this."

"Me too." I nod at her and she joins the stream of kids. Chase and I step into the throng of students as we head to our first class.

"This is all so weird," Chase whispers to me as we walk quickly through the halls.

Talk about an understatement. I just nod, and keep walking. But I totally agree with him. If what he thinks is true. Someone out there is controlling us. Moving us around like chess pieces. Not caring if we get hurt. Or what the outcome of all of this could be.

Right before we enter class Chase stops me. "You okay?"

"No, I'm not. None of this makes sense."

I twist my fingers. I feel tears rising in my eyes. I know that nothing is going to be okay until we understand what is happening.

"How are you feeling?"

"I feel like it's going to be all right." He smiles reassuringly. "And no matter what happens, I sense something in you that screams 'heroine,' so you're going to be all right. Me, on the other hand..." He makes an explosion bomb noise with his mouth.

I laugh and shake my head. "You'll be fine as well, Chase." I bump his shoulder playfully.

He laughs. "I don't know…"

I step into the classroom and say over my shoulder, "Let's hope nothing happens that I have to put that 'heroine' thing to work."

Our morning classes are boring, as usual. All I can think of is the power hidden inside me, the tattoo on my wrist, and the blonde boy behind me who shares the same worries and questions. I also make a point to avoid the bathrooms and water fountains.

Lunch is the usual. Mediocre food, which lies grey and untouched on my plate. The noise of the cafeteria clatters in my ears.

"We should do it now, y'all," Chase leans in and whispers. Ri nods, twisting her long blonde hair.

"Fine. We have to leave one at a time, so we don't bring attention to ourselves." I glance at some teachers standing along the walls. "I'll go first."

"Wait." Chase catches my wrist and pulls me back down. "I can monitor the teachers' thoughts to make sure no one is suspicious."

"Won't that give you a killer headache?" Ri asks.

I nod, "Maybe it would be best if I just left. To save you from the headache."

"I'll be fine," he says, smiling reassuringly. He closes his eyes. A moment passes; then his brow furrows and his hands clench.

"Go. Now," he grits out.

I give him a nervous look, squeeze Ri's shoulder; then stand up, walking briskly away. I check around, making sure no one is watching, before flashing my I.D. card to exit. As soon as I am out of eyesight I take off into a sprint.

I try to shut down the elated feeling of doing something fun and important as I screech around the white halls. Finally, I arrive at the door that leads to the chemistry lab, sliding my I.D. across the lock. The black door slides open silently.

Sitting down on a stool, I twist my fingers, rubbing away some of the stress. This is all too crazy. Are we really about to do this? Experiment on what we could do with this strange new thing that is happening to us? What if I hurt someone? I couldn't live with myself knowing that this had been partly my idea. I stand up and pace as I wait, questions circling my head. What if the others didn't make it? What if they were already found out?

I slide my fingers along the vials of green steaming liquid in the laboratory. The contents move away from my fingers.

Suddenly the door slides open. The noise makes me jump. Ri and Chase enter. Ri clings to Chase's arm.

"Were you followed?" I ask, hurrying over to them.

"I don't think so," Chase says.

He peeks through the window in the door. He looks a little pale. Probably from listening to other people's thoughts.

"Ri, do you mind sealing the door shut?" I ask.

Ri nods and begins running her hand along the seam of the door. Ice creeps out of her fingers, crawling along the metal. Her fingers shake and the ice comes unsteadily.

"How're we going to do this?" she asks, her voice quiet.

"That's what I'm wondering," Chase says with a sigh. "I mean, who wants to volunteer to let me read their mind?"

Ri keeps her hands lowered and mouth shut.

"I'll do it, I guess," I mutter.

It would not be fair to leave him out of all of this. Chase gives a grateful smile.

"Let's move to different corners of the room to practice. Wouldn't want to get caught in the crossfire." Chase and I stay where we are, watching Ri move away. Chase steps up to me and smiles apologetically.

"Sorry about this, I promise you can spray me in the face or something."

"It's okay. I mean, you have to try it eventually." I sit down on the stool again and grab the side of the desk. My knuckles turn white.

"Just get it over with," I whisper and Chase laughs.

"Jeez, El, it's not like I'm performing heart surgery."

"That's true. Please hurry, though."

"Okay, okay, bossy pants." He does not say anymore as he steps forward and places his fingers on my temples.

I raise an eyebrow at him.

"What? It's what they do in the movies from a long time ago."

He shuts his eyes and the room goes silent, other than the small sounds of shattering ice coming from the corner where Ri is practicing. Chase begins to shake and quickly takes his fingers away.

"Whoa, your mind is intense."

He shakes his head, like he is trying to clear a fog.

"Uh, thanks, how kind of y—" My retort is lost as the room begins to shake violently.

Vials rattle on their shelves, some of them dropping to the concrete floor and shattering. There is another noise, like metal snapping and twigs cracking. My head whips up and I spot a dark-haired boy standing in the doorway, roots surrounding him. The door, broken off its hinges. His bright blue eyes go wide as they meet mine.

A crack begins to run along the floor. Chase and I jump back from it as it spreads. He grabs for my hand but misses as I tip backwards when the floor gives a violent shake. Crashing to the ground, my body jarrs from the impact.

The windows shatter, and the glass crashes to the floor, creating a sound like thunder. I cover my head, and feel tiny pricks of glass dig into my skin.

I spot Ri under the shattered windows, her hands over her head. Her mouth is open in a silent scream.

"Ri!" I scream, extending my hand towards her.

Ri cries for me but her shriek is cut short. She's gone. Literally. She's disappeared.

I turn back to yell at the Plant Boy but he's gone too. The only trace that he was ever there are the roots and the broken door.

"Chase, what's happening?" I pick myself off the floor in a last effort to get to him.

I run towards Chase, but slip on the chemicals that have spilled all over the floor. I fall again. The green chemicals burn my fingers.

I reach for Chase, trying to find something to steady me. He tries to grab my hand, terror written all over his face, but something whips him away.

I'm left alone in the chaos. What is happening? Where did they all go?

I lie in a pool of green chemicals, feeling the acid as it burns into my skin, bracing for whatever is going to happen next. Glass shatters. I feel shards prick my hands as I shield my face. Shelves fall.

The ground rumbles more violently. I close my eyes, gritting my teeth. And then everything disappears in a flash of light.

CHAPTER 7

BUBBLES AREN'T THE BEST WEAPONS

The light flashes through my body, my veins. It takes me under, asks me to join it in a warm place full of light. I feel detached from my own body, as if the light has separated me from my very being. It has a cold edge that scares me. Struggling to get free, I find no way out. No way to escape this prison of light.

Once, when I was younger I almost drowned. My school took us to these falls that had been preserved in the wild. It was the greenest, most beautiful place I had ever seen. I leaned over the railing, wishing I could touch the cool mist. I toppled over the edge and into the cold water below. The waterfall took a hold of me and held me there. Never in my life had I felt so trapped. Stuck in a circular motion of death.

I feel the same now, trapped.

It's over, and I am left sprawled on the cold, dark floor of some cave. A cold, lonely cave. A cave full of dripping stalactites. A cave where my worst nightmares could happen.

Light filters through a shaft in the ceiling, letting in just enough light to see. The icy air bites at my skin. My hoodie is in tatters from the acids in the lab. I hug myself, wondering why I didn't wear a coat. Probably because I didn't think I was going to come to this Cave of Doom. My hoodie barely keeps out the stinging air. My knees bang together, the exposed skin covered in scrapes and bruises.

Managing to push myself to my feet, I find that I am alone. In this cavern of shifting lights. With no idea how I got here. Or where I am. Or what to do.

My teeth chatter and I stuff my hands into my hoodie pocket.

My mind calms enough to take in the surroundings and the dire situation that I am in.

I am hopelessly lost and desperately alone.

So I go with the most obvious thing I can think of, "Help!" I pause and cup my hands to my mouth, angling towards the hole in the ceiling.

"I'm stuck down here! Please, help me!"

Nothing, no one. Then suddenly a shift of breath from behind me. A rustle of movement, echoing off the walls.

I shift on my heel, and find myself staring into two giant green eyes. And when I say giant, I mean *giant*. Bulbous and unblinking, with dark, narrow slits for pupils.

I put my hand to my mouth to silence a scream as two curls of steam swirl up and around the green-eyed thing's nose. Sharp yellow teeth glint in the dim light. Yellow saliva drips from its dagger-like fangs. A low growl echoes through its stomach.

A scream claws its way out of my throat and echoes through the cavern, mixing with the growls from the beast.

The beast lets out a roar, huge, ominous, and breathtaking. But not the good kind.

So I do the most logical thing I can think of… again. I turn around and run, not glancing back but know I am being pursued by the beast behind me. Its claws scrape the floor, dangerously close to where my sneakers are hitting the rough stone.

A blast of water from behind me sends me ricocheting into the air and hitting the ceiling that is far above. Pain splinters through my back and head as I collide with stone, stars dance before my eyes. I force away the blackness that creeps into my vision.

Time seems to stop before gravity takes a hold of me. I fall back down towards the ground, which must be at least fifty feet below. I scream and flail for a moment when I see the beast, which I now notice is a *dragon,* that can shoot *water,* and is right below me, poised to swallow me whole. And I have no doubt it could, being the size of a small truck. Apparently, this day *could* get a thousand times worse.

I mean dragons don't even exist, my mind tells me. *Obviously, they do, because this one is about to eat you!*

I close my eyes, sending a plea into the universe before shooting my hands out and harnessing the tingling that is deep in my skin.

Water bursts from my fingers in a geyser, which blasts off the dragon and suspends me in the air, inches from where the dragon's mouth had been. My arms begin to shake from the strain of keeping the geysers streaming out of my hands.

My arms give out, and I fall towards the ground, grateful now that I had halted my fall. Managing to fall into a roll, my legs scream in protest as they hit the hard ground. Needles shoot up my legs and pain explodes in my back.

I manage to jump to my feet, thanking the adrenaline coursing through my veins, just as the dragon takes a swipe at my head. My legs threaten to collapse as I dive out of the way, and I throw a bubble at its open mouth. It's the only thing I can manage to pull out of the water hovering in the air.

Apparently, bubbles don't make the best weapons.

The dragon looks insulted.

Opening its large blue mouth, which is scaled, I notice, water bursts from it in a giant geyser that rivals mine 100 to 1. Somehow, I manage to roll out of the way of the geyser and begin springing down the corridor that will hopefully lead out of this cavern.

And when you get there? my mind asks.

"I'll cross that bridge when I come to it," I answer out loud and pump my arms and legs faster as I race down the tunnel, the dragon close behind.

The dragon doesn't seem too fast, thankfully. You couldn't be, being that large with wings at your sides.

I glance behind me for a moment, and find its large talons inches from my feet.

Apparently, it's fast enough. It could lunge and swallow me whole. My eyes catch on something glinting silver and gold in the distance. A heaping amount of treasure. I sprint to reach it, pouring all of my energy into my run. The cavern opens up into a giant room made of stone. Columns made of silver line the gigantic room.

Yet I don't have time to take in the magnificence because a roar shakes the columns and echoes behind me. I lunge at a black sword hilt sticking out of a mound of gold and silver objects, praying it has a blade at the end of it, trying to not think of the wealth at the end of my fingertips. The dragon snaps its teeth together behind me, knowing its prey is cornered.

Pulling out the sword, I find it does have a blade, and just in time. I spin around and brandish it, just as the dragon reaches me. I point the sword and close my eyes, locking my elbows and my knees.

A shock ricochets through me as a sickening crunch resounds throughout the stone cavern, then silence.

I peel my eyes open one at a time and find the dragon lying before me, the sword sticking out of its mouth. Blue blood soaks my white sneakers and legs, as well as the floor. The sword is buried up to its hilt.

Stop looking, my brain advises.

I fall to my knees and take deep breaths, trying to stop the bile from coming out of my mouth.

"I'm sorry," I whisper to the blue and green dragon, as I lay a hand on its scaly head. "I just didn't want to be your lunch." And with that I grab the sword hilt, and pull it out of its mouth.

CHAPTER 8

THE DESTINY OF MURIEL WILEY

I stumble down the dimly lit passageway, pretty sure I'm going crazy. The fact that all of this just happened is... well...not possible. Sure, I know it just happened because of the blue blood on the sword I am gripping in my hand, and the scrapes and bruises all over my body are real. And the shivers of panic hitting me definitely aren't an illusion.

But, it just wasn't right. Dragons don't exist. And they certainly don't have water powers. Besides, they're supposed to breathe fire, not water.

Of course, it's not real. But that doesn't mean that it didn't happen. Just because I've never seen all of this before, doesn't mean it isn't real.

I don't want this to be real. I don't want to come to terms with the fact that I am alone in a cave with no way to get out. Also, there could possibly be more dragons. And I don't think I'll survive my next encounter.

I shove away my common sense. I am pretty sure that I am just trying to convince myself that it is all fake. My brain is too muddled to try and figure out everything that has happened in the last fifteen minutes. And if I did try to figure all of this out, I think I would short-circuit, and I would die here like the dragon. Lying on the stone, my bones white and abandoned.

And what about my friends? Did this happen to them as well? Are they dead? I can't think of that.

I should have been there to protect Ri. I'm her best friend. Someone she should be able to rely on.Not someone who disappears and leaves her friend alone in a room that's shaking with glass breaking all around her.

Sighing, I pick up my pace. This is all just a crazy dream that feels like it is real life. It will go away.

I should probably stop lying to myself. *The impossible is possible.*

Stumbling, I finally spot light filtering across the floor, playing with the shadows. My heart leaps, I am almost out of here.

I run out into the light and feel the warmth of the sun hit my face. A green forest sprawls before me, no paths of direction to lead me. Songbirds fill the silence.

I begin to walk away and into the woods but a whispery voice stops me in my tracks, "Congratulations, Muriel Wiley, you have completed your test."

Almost jumping out of my shorts, I spin on my heel so quickly I almost fall over. Finding my balance, I aim my sword at a lady, who is dressed in a black gown. Swirls of silver play across the surface of the fabric. Her pale skin glimmers in the dark forest.

"Who are you? What's going on here?" I ask, leveling the sword at her. I hate threatening her, it feels cold and harsh. But now isn't the time for kindness.

"You were put to a test to see if you could be a Protector. Your friends were faced with a trial, as well." She tucks her arms into her wide sleeves. "As for where we are, you are soon to find out. We shall go now. The Leader is waiting."

I pick out two words that are completely foreign to me: Protector and Leader. She said them with importance, like they're names of something great.

"If you do not come with me, Muriel Wiley, I will make you." She raises a delicate eyebrow threateningly. Her dark hair sways in the wind.

"Do you really expect me to just leave with you?" I laugh. "I'm sorry, but I think I'll just leave now..." My nerves tangle around in my stomach. Running into the woods is sounding more and more inviting. As I'm talking, winds bind my hands behind my back, and I float in the air, not able to move or speak. My eyes even seem to be glued in the same position, staring into the grey sky.

"By force, then. We must go see the Leader, Muriel Wiley. This is your destiny."

CHAPTER 9

A PLAYER GOING IN BLIND

A ring is slipped onto my finger, cold and silver, with a wave encrusted on the portion facing my palm.

"This will be your transportation. It is called B.T., which stands for 'Bender Transit.'" The woman tucks her hands deeper into her sleeves. "Every ability has its own ring. You will see the process soon."

I want to speak, but am unable to move anything through the chains of wind binding me. I can hardly even think. Whatever is holding me hostage makes a fogginess fill my head that I can't seem to shake off. The woman takes my hand and pushes down on the wave that is encrusted into the ring.

Instantly, I know I'm in trouble.

My body is breaking down into tiny molecules of... Water? My legs disappear in tiny bubbles. My breaths come short. My body becomes free. I can speak.

"Lady...?"

"It is Lady Dez, actually." She brushes off her dress, making sure it's as pristine as possible. "Do not be afraid, Muriel Wiley. Trust the process. You will not be harmed."

Right. As I *dissolve*. My breaths continue to come short, and I squeeze my eyes shut, unable to watch what is happening to me any longer.

Then I am gone. Literally. Time, thoughts, sound, and sense. All gone. All senses of the present fade away.

Then it all snaps back into place, like a rubber band being pulled and then released. I can hear, feel, smell. I almost pass out from relief.

I add that to the list of the *weirdest things to ever happen to me*. The list seems to be getting longer and longer.

Breathing a sigh of relief, I find that the winds hold me captive again. I had a moment of freedom, but I am a captive once more.

My eyes are frozen in place, focused on a clear blue sky, unlike the grey one we just left behind. Just at the tip of my vision is a gold spire stretching towards the clouds.

"If you do not fight, I shall let you go," Lady Dez whispers in her hushed voice.

Her black dress, accented in starry silver, swishes in the late afternoon breeze.

I mean, what confirmation could she be looking for? I can't move.

Winds whistle. My invisible chains fall away. Suddenly I can move again. I jump to my feet and spin toward Lady Dez, unsure of my next move.

She is way more powerful than I am. And she holds the sword I got from fighting the dragon. I am pretty used to feeling powerless and it's not fun. In my society, there have never been options.

"Please, tell me what is happening," I beg. "I need help... understanding all of this."

She holds all the cards. I'm a player going in blind.

"I transported you from the Unpassable Forest to the Leader's castle, where you shall meet the one who is to foretell your future."

"Huh," is all I say. She raises an eyebrow at me.

None of this makes sense.

"Let us go and meet the Leader and find you some answers."

Oh, I like that last part. Answers are what I need.

I follow behind her as she trails along a stone pathway.

"Do you work for the Leader?" I ask, and stuff my hands into my shredded hoodie pocket.

"I am one of the Leader's Eminences." She says the last word again like it is important, which it probably is. I wish she would explain the mysteries she keeps alluding to.

"Sorry, if you don't mind me asking. Am I dreaming? Is this like an alternate universe, where everything seems super real, but it's not?"

Lady Dez lets out a laugh. "No, Muriel Wiley, this is not a dream. This is your reality, just hidden from your eyes 'til the time was right."

"That makes perfect sense," I say. "Please, just call me El, I'm not really into that formal stuff."

"All right, *El*, it is time to be off. The Leader awaits. Right this way, please." She leads me along an intricate garden path. Golden and sky-blue flowers suddenly appear to make a vine cover over my head, and their scent calms my nerves ever so slightly. I run my hand through their petals. Trails of golden dust stick to my fingertips.

A babbling sound of water meets my ears, and I spot a silver fountain. Splashes of crystal water fall into a calm pool below. Rainbow-colored fish swim in its depths. If I could, I would stay here forever. In this peaceful garden of color.

The fresh breeze brushes my face. The sky is a bright aquamarine. My eyes burn and I swallow tears. I've never been in a place so beautiful, so serene. There is so much color, so much beauty. So much that my Government would hate. So much that they would destroy it if they ever found it.

Four more palaces lay spread on four more clifflike hills. And four more bridges. They stand in a perfect circle, dividing a lush green valley into five triangles. It appears that someone cut up a bunch of pieces of Earth and slammed them down onto this island.

"Why is it shaped like a pie?" I ask.

Lady Dez raises an eyebrow. "Excuse me?"

"The island, it's shaped like a pie."

Lady Dez does her best not to look offended. "Oh, yes. The island is split into different provinces for different working classes. If everything goes well today, you should be able to tour them."

"That would be cool, I think." Right now, what I could really go for are answers to all of the questions bouncing around in my head. "Okay...one thing is off. I know that all of this isn't…natural. And no human has heard of this. So, what's going on here? And why haven't I passed out yet, or something that happens when you go into shock? This is…a lot to take in."

Lady Dez turns back to me, her hands fiddling with her long sleeves. "You are correct, El. We are not human. And I know that this is going to sound shocking, but the reason you are not panicking too badly is that we planted things in your mind to help you settle down when you arrived. Just as we triggered your talent, we have been helping you all along."

"Okay, that is very *terrifying* and *twisted*." I grip my head, maybe I can remove whatever is inside it. "But you didn't answer my question. We aren't human. But what are we?" I lift my head up. I always knew something was different with me. But I had not expected this. Another... world? And I'm not human?

"There is a name, indeed, to all of this. The Leader will explain, as she will explain a lot of things. Just be patient. She will answer your questions."

I let out a long sigh. "Okay...I guess that makes sense. I just really need some answers."

"I understand. Now let us go."

She steps aside and waves her hand, offering for me to go first. I inch closer, unsure of all of this. Unsure of this world that she is hinting at that has existed under the cover of...something. And I'm something different.

Lady Dez leads me out of the pathway and my breath catches in my throat. I am on a steep, rocky cliff. A golden bridge stretches before me, seeming to lead into the unknown. I step back a little, the heights making me suddenly dizzy. The height of the wall back in Ractia pales in comparison.

I press a hand to my cheek and find that it's wet. A sniffle escapes me. Lady Dez doesn't seem to mind. She doesn't even look at me.

"Look around you, El. This is your future and your past," Lady Dez whispers, a smile on her face. I cannot help but believe that this is real, as crazy as it seems.

I step out onto the bridge and it clears beneath my foot, the golden particles moving away from the pressure. I shriek and scuttle back, afraid that I'll fall.

"You could've warned me." Every time I place my hand or foot on the bridge it becomes clear. "Weird," I mutter to myself.

"It is science, El. The light particles move away from the heat of your hand." My eyes widen at her. These beings, or whatever they are, are not just powerful, they are insane science geniuses.

"Okay, I definitely don't want to know how you did that." Lady Dez chuckles from behind me, catching the lie. I *do* want to know.

"It is okay to be curious, El. As you get older you will develop the talent of bending light, just as you do water, which you have not explored very much. That is how you got to the cave. An experienced Flecte transported you there by breaking your body down to light, the way I broke your body down to water. It is the same science, really. The elements call us, and we respond and harness them."

"Eww, don't say 'particles' and 'breaking body' together again, please." I grin at her evilly. "And don't think I didn't notice you calling that thing that brought me wherever we are, a 'Flecte.'"

Lady Dez flushes.

"I might have let it slip. The Leader wishes to tell you everything. I apologize."

I roll my eyes and turn back around, focusing on making it across the Bridge O' Doom alive.

So, I am a Flecte, whatever that means. I am walking on light. That's impossible, right? Also, these people, who claim I am one of them, can break people's bodies down into elements. I mean, it happened to me.

We come to the end of the bridge, and I breathe a sigh of relief. Two statues stand at the end of the bridge. Symbols of a wave, a brain, a gust of wind, a snowflake, and a tree with its roots emblazoned on the sides of each stone pyramid. Spherical suns with their jagged rays top the monoliths. A star perchs on each sun.

Lady Dez leads me along a pathway and points out what the other palaces and pie triangles are for. She points out the other castles. One castle is for people like me, an educational institution for Flectes. The other castles are "classified."

It's all so large and overwhelming. I steady myself on the railing, trying to grasp my situation.

Finally, we arrive at a step, the walk seeming to have lasted forever. A towering golden door, ornamented with a silver sun, separates us from the palace. Lady Dez knocks in an intricate pattern and it swings open to reveal an entryway made of white pearl. Two gold-filigree doors lead into a throne room. Lady Dez swishes in, and I just have time to jump into the castle after her and out of the way of the doors before they bang shut behind me. That was welcoming.

Lady Dez passes the doors and falls to a knee, her head bowed. "She is here, Leader," she says.

Five tall windows stretch toward the ceiling. The light of the setting sun filters in behind a throne made of precious stone. Vines creep towards the ceiling with the same golden flowers bursting among the emerald green.

I step forward and almost fall over my own feet.

Seated on a gilded throne in the center of the room is the most beautiful woman I've ever seen. A glow from her halcyon robe shimmers on her dark skin and lightning-blue eyes. The setting sun glows through an arched window, spilling like liquid amber on her long, dark waves of hair. An aurora of light crowns her head.

The woman smiles, and the whole room lights up, brighter than the sun at its zenith.

My shoulders relax. I am filled with a sense of belonging.

"Welcome, Muriel Wiley, to Zilliad, the Land of Light."

CHAPTER 10

A TICKET OUT OF CRAZY TOWN, PLEASE

"Stop fighting! We will not hurt you!"

A crash from the foyer echoes through the room just as the Leader finishes welcoming me. I whip around, but can't see what is happening. The wall blocks my vision. But whoever is on the other side can't be too happy.

"Ah, your friends are here," the Leader says and rises to her feet gracefully.

She glides off her throne like water spilling on stones, her shimmering robes trailing behind her. She drifts toward the doors and I follow quickly behind her. Curses and smashing noises echo through the room. I wince at a shout of pain. I recognize Ri's voice in the pandemonium.

"Muriel," the Leader says hurriedly, and I turn to look at her. She takes my hands in hers. They are smooth and warm, but also firm.

The Leader and I stand eye to eye as she continues, "I will need you to calm them down. This is a very traumatic experience. Your mind reacted to the comforting trick that a Mind Flecte put on you. They…must not have succumbed to it well, or at all. I am Honora, by the way, and we are so glad you are here at last." She smiles. But I cannot return it, knowing my friends need me. "Fifteen years is a long time to wait for someone you have been hoping would protect you," Honora says, and squeezes my hands. Her right hand is ornamented with the same style of jewelry that is on my wrist tattoo.

I shake my head. I knew that they must have known about us, controlled us, and triggered the powers. But waiting for us?

"You must have it wrong. I can't protect anyone."

Honora smiles gently, knowingly, which only adds to my nerves. She doesn't confront what I said as she releases my hands and says, "We must go comfort your friends."

She turns to Lady Dez, who is standing quietly a few steps behind us, arms tucked in her sleeves. Her white visage, cool and collected as ever. "Come, Dezra, let us help these children."

I follow Honora through the doors into the foyer, which is still echoing with shouts of anger and threats. Chase is swiping punches at a red-haired man, who is dodging easily. Ri has frozen the legs of the man guarding her. She seems to be pressing an icicle to his neck.

The dark-haired boy—the one we saw right before everything shook to pieces—has a man trapped in a cage of roots that squeeze his prisoner tighter and tighter.

"I don't know him," I say, pointing to the dark-haired boy. Honora's brow pinches together.

"That was not supposed to happen, you were all supposed to meet before," Honora says and laces her bronze fingers. Her lightning-blue eyes spark with worry, but only for a second.

"Well, we didn't. Chase and Ri need me. And they are my first priority," I say, watching Ri. I want to help her, to free her from the panic that has taken hold of her.

"Very well," Honora says with a nod. She gestures to the men, who are under attack from Chase, Ri, and the dark-haired boy. "Muriel, meet the rest of my Tribe. They must not have wanted to use magic on their children, unlike Dezra here." She aims a pointed look at Lady Dez, who shrugs, barely raising her eyes from the ground. "Go calm your friends, Muriel. I will take care of the boy."

Honora steps to the side, and I nod. Rushing forward, I go to Ri first and grab her arms, noticing that the ice has reached the torso of the man guarding her. The icicle has just broken his skin.

He grits his teeth. I know he could take her, but he doesn't want to use his powers on Ri. I pull Ri back and force her to look at me.

"Ri! Calm down! They want to help us. They're not here to hurt you."

Her eyes focus on me, fear deep in her irises. Her hair drips with silver droplets of water. "They messed with our heads, El, and stuck me in the middle of a storm right in the middle of an ocean to see if I was 'strong enough' to be a 'Protector.' I have every right not to be calm!" she snaps, but the ice ebbs away from the man's legs and the icicle pulls back.

"They stuck you in the middle of an ocean?" I ask, terrified. Maybe the dragon wasn't as bad as it had seemed.

"Not just an ocean, a stormy, wild ocean. I had to freeze paths through it to get to the shore, which was like three hundred yards away." She shudders and places her head in her hands.

Her voice is muffled as she says, "It was the longest nine-hundred feet of my life."

"I bet," I whisper, wishing I could comfort her more, but Chase needs to be calmed now.

I feel selfish as I say, "Ri, I need you to be strong for me. I know there's a lot going on, but these people are going to answer some of our questions." I force a smile and say again, "They want to help us."

She nods slowly, and releases the man completely. I smile at her sadly and rush toward Chase, who has finally landed a punch on his captor's face, leaving an impressive red mark.

"Chase!" I yell.

He spins around toward me. Eyes bloodshot and wild. I screech to a stop when I notice his glazed eyes. He looks at me, but doesn't even seem to see me. I have to help him escape his mind, which has turned into a maze consisting only of dead ends.

He throws a punch at me. I dodge out of the way, tackling him to the ground and dragging him away from his captor, all in one move. Maybe fighting on the streets of Ractia taught me something: how to escape. I pin Chase as he continues to fight.

"Chase, it's me!" I yell.

His glazed eyes clear of the fog covering them. "El?" His arms relax beneath my fingers. I release him. "My head." He clutches his head like he's trying to get something––or someone––out.

"What happened?" I ask, sitting down next to him. He turns his eyes toward me. They are speckled with red. Like drops of blood in a stormy ocean.

"They filled my mind with something, some darkness." He grips his wavy blond hair, which is drenched in sweat. "I'll never forget the feeling."

"Oh," I whisper. I reach out and awkwardly pat his leg, hoping I'm being comforting. "I'm sorry."

He shrugs and picks himself off the ground, offering me a hand to pull me up. He hoists me to my feet and drops his hand back to his side. I rub my arm.

"I'll live. You, on the other hand, look like you got chewed up and spit out." He cracks a grin.

"I did, sort of. I had to battle a dragon. And almost got eaten—twice. I also fell from fifty feet in the air, and just managed to stop myself from being dragon food by using geysers that erupted from my hands. It's something I definitely don't want to do again."

"Hopefully we'll never have to almost die again," he says with a laugh.

I grimace. "For some reason, I doubt that this will be the last time."

He nods, and almost says something else, but Honora interrupts him.

"Come, children, it is time to meet your fourth tribe member." Chase and I share a look.

This is going to be fun.

The dark-haired boy is in a prison of ice and he does *not* look happy. A man with a tattoo just like Ri's, holds his hand against the ice prison. The ice pulses blue where his hand touches it.

"Welcome to Zilliad, Ty Ramenoff."

The boy's eyes darken, he watches us nervously. "Thanks, but no thanks," he says, glowering. "Can I catch the train out of Crazy Town, please?"

I have to agree with him. Getting a ride out of here would be wonderful. Forgetting that this ever happened and returning to normal life is sounding more and more appealing.

But do I really want to go back? All I've ever wanted was an escape.

"This is your Tribe, or most of it." Honora smiles at the four of us. Then nods at Chase, Ri, and I. "Introduce yourselves."

"I'm Muriel, but please call me El." I crack a grin. "And if you find tickets out of Crazy Town, let me in on them, please."

Ty cracks a small smile, his teeth white against his olive-toned skin. "I'll make sure to let you know," he says, sounding slightly relieved.

"I'm Chase Cutler, and I'll take a ticket as well." Chase smiles, and it calms me to see part of his carefree self return.

"And I'm Ri Simons." Ri shuffles her feet, clenching and unclenching her fists. She doesn't add to our joke. Her eyes are wild, unfocused.

I take her hand and squeeze it.

Ty eyes all of us, his lips are becoming blue from the frozen prison surrounding him. "I guess we're in this together, then."

I nod solemnly.

And Chase mutters, "I guess so."

The room becomes silent. Lady Dez clears her throat, and Honora says, "Let us go to the throne room."

Honora waves at the man that is fueling Ty's prison, signaling for him to release Ty. The ice dissolves as the man removes his hand. Ty glances down at his dripping clothes, then up at us. He smiles widely. The corners of his golden brown eyes, crinkling. "Can you help me with this?" he asks, gesturing to my tattoo then to his dripping clothes.

"Oh," I say, taken aback. "Sure." I wave my hand and pull the water out of his clothes. It forms a bubble, and I stare at it for a moment. My only thought is, *there must be something seriously wrong with me.* I disperse it by pulling it into tiny bubbles till it finally evaporates. I smile sheepishly and Chase gives a sarcastic round of applause.

"I did not know you had so much control, Miss Wiley," Lady Dez says, bowing her head slightly.

"Um…yeah, I guess. It's just a feeling." I twist my fingers and turn back to Ty. "How did you find us? At school, I mean?"

We begin to follow Honora, Lady Dez, and the four men, into the throne room.

"I saw you all talking and then you snuck off. I had been on edge because of—" he pauses to glance at his wrist, where a tattoo with a tree with twisting roots is imprinted, "—all of this. I was watching, seeing if anyone else had had it happen to them. Sure enough, there you three were. You weren't very good at being secret, you all looked pretty guilty."

"Whoops," Chase says.

"And then I followed you once you left the cafeteria, and as soon as I saw the ice creeping up the door, I knew that you were all like me. Or somewhat like me."

"Huh," I say.

Ri blushes. "Sorry I got us followed," she whispers to me.

I shrug. "It's okay, it was bound to happen. It doesn't really matter now, anyways. I mean, we aren't even on the same continent that we were thirty minutes ago. Clearly we have bigger things to worry about."

We aren't in Ractia anymore. And nothing will ever be the same. Not after we know that this exists. How will I keep this from Rolia?

Honora settles herself on the throne again, and the three men and Lady Dez stand at her side, two on each side of the throne.

"We have decided to allow you each a couple of questions. I know this must be very scary and new, and it would only be fair," Honora says.

"No kidding," Ty mutters from beside me, rage clear on his face. He speaks louder, "I have two questions. What is a Protector? And why did *we* have to suffer through trials?"

"Those are two very valid questions, Ty Ramenoff, and I will answer them to my best ability," Honora says, shifting on her throne. "What I am to tell you will not be easy to hear, but you asked, and you shall receive. Five children were created to become Protectors. And when we saw our world becoming dark, we decided to have you born and planted with the humans until we needed you. The trials were to see if you were strong enough.

And since you are all here, you have proven that you are strong enough."

"Because we didn't die," Chase snarks.

"I am truly sorry. But there are more trials to come, sadly. And you will be tested when you go to school. And at last, the five of you will become the team you were meant to be," Honora says.

Go to school? Here? How will that work with Rolia? She'll be asking so many questions whenever I disappear.

I'm about to voice my concerns when Chase says, "I'm sorry to say this, lady, but there are only four of us." He caught something I hadn't noticed. Maybe it's because I am worried about how my robotic mother will handle all of this.

"Ah, yes," Lady Dez says, stepping forward. "My son, Devlyn is your fifth Tribe member, a Wind Flecte. He was raised here when I asked for a son."

I'm taken aback by her words. Why couldn't that have happened to us? The four of us had to be thrown into the broken human world. While this Devlyn got to wear gold and live in a castle.

Lady Dez continues, oblivious to my discomfort and rage. "Dev is very excited to meet all of you. He has been without a Tribe for the last fifteen years, when he should have been training with them like the rest of the children." She steps back into place and Honora nods at her.

The four of us haven't had any training either. So he won't be too out of place.

"Thank you, Dezra." Honora says, looking pointedly at all of us. Waiting for our next questions.

I decide to ask the next question. I'm afraid I might pass out, or empty my stomach of my skimpy lunch before I can voice some of the questions rattling around in my head.

"Okay, about this Tribe thing you keep mentioning, what is it? And Flectes? Where did they come from?"

"A tribe is a group of five gifted Flectes who work and fight together. Whenever the Leader Tribe—" she pauses, gesturing to herself and the four people standing next to her, "—fall out of leadership after a hundred years, another group is voted in. The strongest of the five is made the Leader. You all have that chance, being Protectors. We have never had children like you."

Children like you. She says it with mystery. Was there more to us that we don't know yet?

"About the Flectes, who we also sometimes refer to as Benders before we gain our ability and for school subjects. Our history is less than bright. We once lived with humans, but they became jealous of our long life and abilities. They tried to harness us, use us for themselves. So our ancestors locked us away on this island, to save us from human greed. The Shadow Flectes, our brothers, were locked in here, too, when the island was larger. Then a civil war erupted. Our kings and queens of old were massacred by a force more powerful and more evil than you can imagine. The island split itself in two, casting away the Shadow Flectes to the East and us to the West."

"That's...a lot more to take in," I mutter. On top of finding out that I was bred to protect these people, this is too much to handle.

Ri steps forward, her lips trembling. "You say we are to live here? That all of this is our destiny, that we are to leave our families for the rest of our lives. You think we will just listen? I want to know how you hold this power to control our lives." She narrows her cold grey eyes.

"You are secured here by the powers that the kings and queens of old secured us with. Once you come, you can never escape," Honora says, tucking her graceful dark fingers into her robes.

I shrink back. Fear rolls in my stomach. This much power should not be held by anyone.

Honora continues, "You belong here. It is your destiny. Your family knew all of this. Muriel is different because she was raised by a robot, who agreed to help, as well. Once you leave them, they will forget they had you. The robot…is going to be trickier. She will have to be erased."

My stomach clenches. Rolia? Erased? She can't be. She was the only one in my life that had ever loved me. It does feel good to know that my human parents hadn't left me in the rain.

"You can't hurt her," I whisper, and Honora gives me a sad look and shakes her head.

"It was her choice," she answers.

Chase places a hand on my shoulder.

"She knew?" I ask, my voice barely audible. She had lied to me. I twist my fingers, tighter and tighter.

Honora nods solemnly. "We are truly sorry about this, Muriel."

"Okay, that's fine. It's fine." But it isn't. This changes everything. She lied to me. The knife of betrayal buries itself into my heart. It makes me want to punch something and lie down and cry till I can't cry anymore.

I turn to the others and they are equally pale. Our parents didn't choose us. They didn't even have to care. I guess I am going to have to get used to the feeling of being an experiment.

"Sorry, I'm going to be demanding, since you're shoving a lot of things down our throats. Number one, we're going to school here? Number two, who are we going to live with? Number three, what's with the 'after one hundred years?' Most people don't live that long. And number four, this is a bonus question, what's with the gold?" Chase asks, keeping his hand on my shoulder. Either to steady him, or steady me.

"Yes, you will go to school in the Ruby level, which is level three. As for where you are to live, we have found a couple families that will take you in."

"We're living with random people, as well as in a random world? Gee, that's great," Chase interrupts.

"They are very kind, all of them. And if it does not work out, you can live in a dorm." Chase shrugs. "As to your third question, we're immortal."

And with that, Ri passes out cold on the floor.

"Oh joy," Chase says, looking at his hands, probably thinking that they won't ever wrinkle. "So that makes you how old?"

"One thousand."

"Of course. I think I need a breath of air." He crumples to the ground right next to Ri.

"I was afraid of that," Honora says. She turns to Ty and me. "Would you two like to hear what the gold means?"

I glance at my crumpled friends, wishing I was with them instead of remaining awake and knowing that all of this is happening. And there is no going back. So I nod.

More information won't kill me, right? Ty nods as well, his almond shaped eyes clouded with fear. Dirt smears his weary face.

"It is the color of our royalty. It harkens back to the days of the Estrella, the kings and queens of old who died in that massacre. We have kept the color as a tribute. The stars are very important to us, and a large part of our culture." Lady Dez and Honora exchange glances. Nervous glances. "You will learn why in the future, I am sure. But now your questions are up. And it is time to say goodbye to your families."

My stomach drops. The air around me squeezes in my lungs. Stars fill my vision. Goodbye? I'm no good at goodbyes.

"Press on the rings that were gifted to you and they will carry you back to your homes. The forces of magic will bring you back after ten minutes. Just call out 'home' when you press it."

If I don't listen, I will never see Rolia again. Just because she lied to me does not mean I get to hold a grudge. A tear slips down my cheek, the beginning of what I fear will be many more to come. I nod at Honora and glance at Ty, who gives me a sad smile. Then finally, I press my ring and call for home.

CHAPTER 11

THE SHADOWS SAY HELLO

I am spit out onto my living room floor. The dull colors feel odd to my eyes after all of the extravagance in Zilliad. I suck in a deep breath and grasp my stomach, forcing myself not to throw up on the carpet. Dissolving and reforming is hard on the body, it'll take a lot to get used to it.

Well, to get used to any of this.

"It's happening, isn't it?" a robotic voice says from behind me.

I spin on my heel and find Rolia sitting on her tracks in the middle of the room. Her eyes are droopy ovals, like they always are when something bad happens. But normally, it's when something goes wrong at school. Not me leaving forever to a strange land and her getting... I can't even finish the thought.

All thoughts of her betrayal leave my mind. She's always been there for me. Now I need to be there for her.

I rush across the room and fall to my knees, wrapping my arms around her oval-shaped body. Tears begin to fall as a desperate hopelessness clenches my chest. Not being able to form words I just sit there, tears streaming down my cheeks, hugging her tightly. Understanding that it will be the last time.

"I'm sorry I lied to you, El," she says, and pats my back with a pronged hand.

"I forgive you," I manage to choke out. "You did what was best. But they're going to hurt you, Rolia." I squeeze her tighter, not willing to let go. Her head rotates slowly, sadly.

"Not 'they' El, 'me.'"

I lean back and look into her downcast eyes. "You can't be serious," I say, remaining on my knees.

I cannot lose anything else today. Not when I was about to lose my reality. Not when everything is falling apart.

I know eventually it will fall back together. But having Rolia out there, caring for me even if I was not with her, would have helped. My stomach balls into knots.

"I am serious. If they found the information that I hold in my database about you, He would wipe out everything you will know. The Flectes will end. And that is not acceptable."

"Who's he?" I ask, clutching her pronged hand.

"The King of the Shadows."

Fear spirals through me, like a bolt of electricity. Just the name is enough to give me chills.

"Now is not the time, El. I must go. The Flectes will protect you, and you will protect them. This is the only way."

"There's so much to say," I whisper, holding her closer. "But I guess I'll have to settle with a thank you."

I know Rolia will destroy herself before she lets anything happen to the Flectes or to me. She's programmed, and can't feel emotion. But she can cause it. My heart throbs in my chest.

I will just have to sit here. And let it happen before my eyes.

"Don't go," I plead, cupping her round head in my hands.

"Goodbye, El." Her eyes blink out, darkness clouds the room, a loud beep echoes, making me jump. Dark oil slips through her seams.

"No!" I scream, my hands slipping in the oil. "Don't leave me!"

I place my forehead where her eyes were normally blue and alive. I sob into the cold metal of her round head.

"I can't do this without you."

Sobs rack my body. My tears mix with the oil. But she remains cold and silent.

Self-destruct in ten seconds.

"No!" I sob, this was definitely getting worse.

9….

I wipe away my tears as I flip her over.

8….

I scramble through the oil and find the hatch hidden on her back.

7….

I punch the metal.

6…5…4….

The flap slips open and I reach around the wires until I find it. Her database chip.

3….

Too many seconds have escaped me.

2....

"Goodbye, Rolia."

1....

I dive behind the couch as an explosion rocks the room. I squeeze my eyes shut, trying to block everything out. Then the room goes dead silent.

Slipping the chip into my pocket, I push myself to my feet, using the couch to steady me. Ashes float to the ground in the center of the room. Clenching my fists at my side, I walk around my house, running my hands along the walls that were the structure of my childhood. This is the only place I have ever known.

I head back into the living room and collapse next to the ashes, pressing my hands into the carpet. My skin tingles as water streams out of my hands, surrounding me and the ashes and my past. I watch as I begin to dissolve. To fade away. Into tiny particles.

But then everything freezes. A chill wind sweeps through the air. A shadow wraps around my body.

I can't escape. My body that was dissolving a second ago reforms in a cold flurry. A voice slithers into the room, a raspy, shadowy voice.

"Hello, Muriel." The voice is deep and dark. Like a cave filled only with shadows.

"Light, help me," I plead.

All I need in this moment is some light. I flex my wrists, trying to escape the bonds holding me. A shadow fills the door. A dark crown on its cowled head.

"I just thought I would interrupt you and say hello." The figure in shadows bows its hooded head.

"Go away," I rasp.

The shadows are taking over. The room is dark. Tears are spilling down my cheeks. Pain like hot needles stabbing my skin.

"Well, I'm not trying to be impolite. I just wanted to see if you were a worthy opponent." The shadow comes closer.

I flinch.

"Who are you? What do you want with me?" I ask, noticing the shadows have loosened ever so slightly. I wiggle, trying to free myself.

"Who am I?" The hooded figure chuckles, a dark sound in a dark room. "I'm your worst nightmare."

"Well then, you should have watched for the wakeup call." I jump to my feet and thrust my arms out. A tidal wave rushes in front of me and drenches the hooded figure.

I run for the back door, but stumble as the wave breaks through the front room and shatters the windows and concrete of the wall. Pain spreads through my hands as I fall hard to the concrete floor of my kitchen. I can't stay down now. Now is the time for survival.

Get up, Muriel!

I jump to my feet and run out the back door. I jump over some concrete blocks and my legs feel like springs. There is a strange rush in my ears and I soar through the air and onto the roof of a house across my backyard. I land in a crouch and shake my head. What just happened?

"Muriel Wiley, this was supposed to be a friendly greeting." The voice reverberates around me.

"I'm sorry, you should have brought flowers if you wanted this to be civil."

The shadowed figure rises above the peak of the roof I am crouching on. His hood has fallen away, revealing a face that will forever haunt my nightmares. His eyes are black, his skin ghostly white. And his hands. Long white fingers covered in scars.

"I will let you go, for now." A wicked grin twists his pale lips. "Until the next time we meet, Muriel Wiley."

"There won't be a next time." I press my ring and shout for Honora.

CHAPTER 12

THE GUARDIANS

As I reform, I realize I am not in the castle with Honora. Everything has gone too wrong today. I've lost my robotic mom, found out that I'm not actually human, discovered there is another realm, killed a dragon, and had a strange encounter with an eerie shadow being. No wonder I can hardly think about anything besides the shadows that keep creeping into my mind.

The room I am in is circular, walls covered in ancient-looking books. The floor is made of dark stone. A desk sits right in front of two square windows that face out onto a busy street bustling with people dressed in fine clothes.

I notice Chase is here, standing next to the bookshelves on my right, head in his hands, shoulders sagging.

"Chase?" I ask, as gently as possible.

His head whips up, eyes puffy and red. Tears make tracks down his bronze cheeks. I take a tentative step forward. Then another. I grab one of his cold shaking hands and pull him over to a small couch. The cushions are soft and silky. I sink into them.

"Is there anything I can do to help?" I ask.

Pain, guilt, and fear are strangling me. But I have to be strong for Chase too. He needs me to be strong right now. His sea blue eyes ripple with fresh tears. He shakes his head.

"You can cry, El."

As soon as he says it, I realize that I need his strength too.

"I don't need t—" I can't even get the sentence out. My body begins shaking as I sob. "Why did this have to happen to us?" I splutter, not even having a coherent thought to be embarrassed.

Holding it in has just made it worse. I can no longer support myself as the rage and loneliness grip me. I slump to the floor, slipping off of the couch. I hear rustling as Chase sits down beside me.

He doesn't do anything for a moment, then sighs and guides my head to his knee so that I won't be laying on the cold stone as I let the tears fall. These few hours have felt like years. Was it only this morning that I had met Chase on the bus?

"Thanks," I say as I wipe my eyes. Taking deep breaths to calm my racing heart, I pull back, realizing how close we are.

"Anytime," Chase assures me and wipes his own tears away. "Why were you late?"

Fear shocks me again. "A person, clothed in shadows."

I can barely get the words out. It's like fear is strangling me again. Shadows begin to cloud my mind once more.

Chase's eyebrows knit together. "What do you mean?"

"Someone doesn't want us here," I whisper.

"Who?" Chase presses.

I shake my head, almost unable to say anything. But I manage to get out, "The King of Darkness. Or shadows."

"That doesn't sound o—" His words are cut off when four people bang into the room.

I jump to my feet, ready for a fight. Shadows black out my vision. I shake my head, trying to clear the fear that is taking hold of me.

But then I come to the realization. They're our new guardians. Yet, this just brings on another wave of panic. How am I supposed to do this?

"Hello, darlings," a young woman ventures. I clear my throat before I am able to speak.

"Hi," I say.

Chase manages a small wave. His ability to speak appears to be frozen by fear.

"We are your new um…," One of the men starts to say. He seems unsure of what to call himself and the rest of them.

"We are so glad you are here," another man says, breaking into a wide grin. He looks like me, tall, dark hair, green eyes.

"I'm Orabelle, and I will be your guardian, if you choose, Chase," a petite, gentle-voiced woman says from the back.

Talk about pressure. I could never say no to someone that delicate.

She steps forward and takes his hands. He flinches slightly but doesn't pull away. A man dressed in black steps forward.

"And I'm Rowan, we are so happy to have you."

"Shall we get going?" Orabelle whispers.

Chase nods timidly and walks forward. He casts me a grin and a thumbs up as the door swings shut behind him. Leaving me alone. With my new *parents*.

"Um," I say, making it twenty times more awkward. I've never really interacted with adults outside of school.

"I'm Harlyn," the lady who first spoke says, breaking into a glowing smile. She is strangely beautiful. But her blonde hair is tinted with grey, which should be impossible, since we're apparently immortal.

"And I'm Blaze. We know this must be terrifying, and we are here to help with anything you need."

"Thank you," I manage to choke out. "I'm Muriel, but please call me El."

"Muriel, that's a beautiful name. And if you'd like to be called El, then it will happen." Harlyn says with a wink of her sky-blue eyes.

"Should we get going?" Blaze asks, offering me a hand.

I take it, my hand shaking. Managing a shaky nod, I follow after their elegant forms. My tattered clothes feel like rags compared to theirs. They wait outside for me as I close the door behind us.

"You've used a B.T. right?" Harlyn asks as she dusts off her sea-green gown.

I nod, twisting my fingers. Traveling with the B.T. has been less than fun.

"Then this will be easy. Just allow us to carry you, and focus on the word we call, okay? We wouldn't want you to be lost in the Light Realm."

I laugh nervously. "Um...ye-yeah. That doesn't sound too fun."

Harlyn smiles reassuringly and takes my hand as she calls out, "Hearthstone."

CHAPTER 13

HEARTHSTONE

The same thing happens as it has the last three times I have traveled in this way. I break down, feel a little icky, then reform. Every time I come back, I run my hands along my torso and legs just to make sure I'm all there still. I don't think I will ever get used to this, though it does seem to be getting easier each time.

We arrive in front of a two -story marble manor. Windows stretch to the roof, gleaming in the fading light. Green fields spread out around us. Blood-red roses and towering trees with gleaming white flowers line the path.

I drop Harlyn and Blaze's hands when I realize I'm still clinging to them. I flush. They don't seem to notice. The air is fresh and crisp, with a hint of salt, reminding me I'm not far from the coast.

Blaze says, to my surprise, "We hope you will be able to call it home someday. I hope, we hope, that you'll be happy here."

Home. This is not my home. It's back in Ractia, California. Yet that isn't home either, not really. I don't belong anywhere. I am stuck between worlds, like a fly in a spider's web.

A sparkling fountain stands in a white stone courtyard in front of the entrance, which is made of beautifully crafted gold. Blaze places his hand at the center of the door and it swings open silently, revealing an entryway that is *very* clean. Cleaner than my house ever was. *Was.* The word makes my heart drop further in my chest.

"We will add your handprint to the doorway," Blaze explains and continues forward, beginning to ascend some stairs.

An archway to the right reveals an elegant sitting room, adorned with blown-glass chandeliers. It reflects different prisms on the walls when the light from a small circular window hits it just right. There is a large, unlit fireplace. Another archway straight ahead opens to the kitchen, and to the left is a third archway, leading to a library, which makes me grin in anticipation.

All of the architecture is crafted from marble. However, the pristine furniture is crafted from all different types of fabrics and woods. Red roses are in golden vases, adding a vibrant splash of color to the room.

Harlyn leads us forward to a twisting elegant stairway.

"You are welcome to read anything in the library as long as you get the all clear from us. And the kitchen is always open to whatever you might need."

"Thank you," I say quietly, twisting my ring around and around my finger.

We continue up the stairs and arrive at one large landing with three doorways, one of which, I'm assuming, leads to Harlyn and Blaze's bedroom.

A large room on the other side of the room appears to be made up of their office and a small library. Scrolls with fancy inscriptions rest on their desks. I would probably get into trouble for touching them, and worse for reading them.

Having flesh-and-blood parents is going to be weird. But at least they're kind. I notice a picture of Harlyn with a unicorn on the wall.

"Unicorns?" I ask.

I already knew there were dragons. But this was news. What else is out there?

"Yes, I have two out back. Blaze has a fascination with dragons. He even helps with some of the ones kept down in Crofter. The dragons are kind of his hobby. Anyways, the unicorns, Violeta and Blissia are a part of my therapy." Harlyn shuffles her feet. Blaze and her share a look.

Something is wrong with Harlyn. And it probably has to do with her hair turning grey. I decide not to ask.

"We have a new unicorn. We...bought her for you."

"Oh wow, thanks. That's really cool," I say, the fact that they got me a unicorn is...different. I've never gotten a gift in my life. Let alone a unicorn. "How long have you known I was coming?"

"About a week," Blaze says, and tells me no more.

I had assumed that they would have been alerted yesterday, which is when Honora triggered my power. Yet they must have started the process beforehand.

Further down a winding hallway a room opens up. Silky curtains are pulled back to reveal a large room. The room takes up half of the top level, which is three times the size of my old room. Huge windows show the beautiful sprawling estate. A large canopy bed, fit for a princess, stands to the right.

To the right of the bed are two bookshelves and a desk. Thick books line the shelves. On the chair, which is pulled halfway out, is a pile of neatly folded clothes ranging in colors of red, black, and white. A satchel is slung over the arm of the chair.

"Your school supplies," Blaze explains when I wrinkle my nose in confusion.

Blaze moves to the right of the room, which has two doors. He opens the one on the left and I find a huge wardrobe, filled with colorful clothes trimmed with frills and lace.

"Is that all for me?" I ask, shocked. I will be able to wear color. This is going to be new.

"Yes," Harlyn says, smiling at my excitement.

The next door over is a bathroom. A giant bathtub and shower stand to the right, and a vanity to the left. The last doorway they show me leads to an inside garden. There, purple and silver flowers, as well as roses, bloom.

"This is really all for me?" I ask again, finding it hard to comprehend. I have always been stuck with a small grey room and a robot for a mom. I shiver at the reminder of Rolia.

"Yes, is it okay?" Harlyn asks, sounding worried. "We can go shopping in Gildalynn if you don't like what we have given you."

"It's *amazing*!" I say as I flop onto my bed. Sure, losing everything was hard, but living here was going to make it a bit easier. I hate myself for such a selfish thought, but I can't help it. If only Rolia were here this would be paradise.

The reminder that I left Rolia makes my stomach flop and my heart squeeze in a painful way.

"Well, we will leave you to get settled. Would you like to meet Blissia in a bit?" Harlyn asks, shuffling towards the door with Blaze. They look nervous, like I'm a wild beast they don't quite know how to deal with.

"Who's Blissia?" I ask.

"Your unicorn."

"Oh, right. Of course."

They leave with smiles. A unicorn. A whole room to myself with a garden.

Harlyn and Blaze are nothing like Rolia. And maybe that's a good thing. The less they remind me of Rolia the better.

But that doesn't mean it doesn't hurt. It hurts more knowing that she knew. Knew that I'd be leaving. Knew I'd be ripped away from her. Knew that she would have to destroy herself.

The past is in the past. It's time to move on. That doesn't mean I will not mourn. That I will not cry. This is my new reality, one that I need to adapt to.

I get up and wander about my room. Reading the covers of the books, which are in a loopy silver writing that isn't English. Yet I can somehow understand what is written.

Just more information that was planted in my mind.

I also explore the garden, picking flowers and putting them by my bed.

When I'm done with that, I venture into the closet. Even the dullest clothes I can find still have intricate details. At the back there is a rack as tall as I am, filled with shoes in all sorts of colors.

I pick a loose green tunic with silver butterfly buttons and pair it with beige pants and brown boots. I decide to start out slow with the colors. If I go too quickly the freedom will not be as sweet.

I tie my hair into a ponytail as I go downstairs. I pad into the kitchen and find Harlyn and Blaze sitting at a large table. Blaze is reading a magazine with dragons on the cover. Guess Harlyn was right about the "dragon obsession."

"You ready?" Harlyn asks, smiling broadly, twisting the strands of her grey hair.

I nod. We head out the back door. I follow her along a grassy lane. Ahead of us is a square building made of some kind of twisted roots, which somehow form a structure. Purple flowers burst over the dark vines covering the enclosure.

"The flowers help calm them," Harlyn explains and plucks a flower off the vines. She hands it to me and I take a sniff. Instantly my heartbeat slows and the urge to fall asleep pulls me down.

"That's intense," I say, and put the flower behind my ear.

My unicorn's name is Blissia, but I shorten it to Miss Bliss, which isn't really shortened, but I prefer it. Blue highlights curl through her mane. And her coat shimmers with silver flecks. She is definitely beautiful. And nothing like I've ever seen before. I'm guessing that this is how I will feel for a while. Totally in awe, and totally confused.

Harlyn teaches me how to groom her and she tells me stories of times she's fallen off. I find myself laughing. We put Bliss and Violeta, Harlyn's unicorn, back in their stalls and walk back up to the house.

"Thank you," I say, smiling. "That was really…nice."

"Of course." She smiles. "Now, it is time for you to see the world that is your rightful home."

CHAPTER 14

THE ADDITION TO THE HALLAWELLS

We head back to my room. Harlyn tells me all about Ravenscroft, which is the school I will be attending. She finishes with a happy sigh, then says, "First we will go to Gildalynn to get your uniforms. I know someone especially good at making them there. Then we can head to Tethoris, which sells your books and other supplies. We can also grab some food, if you'd like."

"It's always a yes to food," I say with a grin. Glancing at the desk, which holds some clothes and books, I ask, "Aren't those what I need?"

Harlyn laughs. "You really want to wear the same uniform every day? No, you need different styles. As for the books, those are just for fun, some of the suggested reads. We received the list of classes you will be taking today, so now we must buy your books."

The mention of school makes my stomach flop.

I've always worn the same two outfits to school. One of which is now in the wastebasket of my new room. I don't need it anymore, and I'll never be going back to Ractia, anyway.

"Oh, thanks," I say, flushing a little.

I will have to get used to the Flectes' extravagant ways. Harlyn ushers me into my closet, mumbling how we need to make a good first impression as a family. She bustles back out with an elegant ruffled green dress and golden slippers covered in emeralds.

"There you go." She lays them on my bed and places her hands on her hips and gestures for me to go into the bathroom to change.

I scoop up the dress and shoes, which both almost weigh as much as I do, making me trip on my way to the bathroom. The dress is surprisingly comfortable, made of a soft emerald silk. The shoes slip onto my feet and adjust to fit my size.

I swish out, and Harlyn gasps, a happy look on her face. "Gorgeous."

I blush bright red, my fingers itching to be twisted.

Harlyn claps her hands. I have a feeling I'll be playing dress up more often.

"We need to go now, it's been a long day for you and you probably would like to crash into bed soon."

I nod, the sunlight has almost completely faded. "Bed does sound nice. But I want to explore, too, so bed can wait."

Harlyn beams and slides her arm through mine. "Let us go then."

We get Blaze from the kitchen, where he still sits reading his dragon magazine. Harlyn ushers us outside and calls, "Golden Petal Avenue!"

A bright street comes into view as we re-form. I now know why it's called Golden Petal Avenue. Leaves and flowers climb up every surface they can touch, sparkling golden in the evening light. The petals form star-like shapes as they curve up and around the golden surfaces.

"Wow," I breathe, releasing Harlyn's hand. Blaze and Harlyn smile at me, loving my awe at their colorful world.

"How did you find so many things to make this place so…wealthy?"

Blaze chuckles lightly. "The mines in the mountains surrounding us are very abundant in what they produce. As for these flowers, Plant Flectes take a special pride in them. They like to bedazzle places."

I laugh at that. Talk about an understatement!

We follow Harlyn down the cobbled street, our shoes clacking against the stone. There are shops lining the streets and other Flectes in midnight blue gowns.

"What's with the colors of the clothes?" I ask, noticing that Harlyn and Blaze also wear midnight blue. I'm the odd one out in my emerald green.

"It is just a way to show class. You saw how the Leader wore Gold, midnight blue is the Reverence. Gildalynn is a town for people who work directly under the Leader."

"That's…slightly confusing," I say, and Blaze breaks into a grin.

"You will understand it eventually."

We come to a small boutique. Golden words splay across the front window. *Snips and Silks.* A wooden door made of twisted roots stands out against the sparkling building.

Harlyn pushes through the door, smiling widely. "You're going to like this place."

Rows upon rows of clothes line the wall. Different styles of shoes make up the back wall. An intricately made desk of interwoven roots stands in the middle of the room. Two changing rooms are on the left. Harlyn steps up to the counter and rings the bronze bell that sits on the well-loved desk. A petite lady, with gold-rimmed glasses steps up to the counter, smiling brightly.

"Hello, Harlyn dear," she says, smiling enough to make wrinkles form around her eyes. Tiny golden owls glint from the corners of her glasses.

"Jane," Harlyn says, smiling. Jane comes around the desk and hugs Harlyn around the waist. She walks with a slight limp.

"We're here to get our new resident a couple of uniforms for level three at Ravenscroft. She is new to... this area. Jane, this is Muriel Wiley." Harlyn stumbles over what she should call me, and I flush. Jane walks up to me and clasps my hand, it's warm and calloused.

"Welcome to Zilliad, darling." She smiles at me and I nod my head in a slight bow.

"Thank you, ma'am."

"Just call me Jane," she says, patting my hand. "Now let's get you some Ruby Level uniforms."

I notice a chart on the side of the desk, reading off the different levels.

Amethyst, level 1. Aquamarine, level 2. Ruby, level 3. Emerald, level 4. Diamond, level 5.

"Won't I be loads behind?" I ask, to no one in particular. Worry wrenches my stomach. It will already be a huge challenge being the new girl. Then also the one who knows nothing? That will be too much to bear.

"Oh, honey, don't worry about it. Levels one and two are mainly about history and boring subjects. You aren't allowed to get into the interesting stuff, like using your abilities and Irradiation Bending and Astronomy and Planetary Science, until you enter level three," Jane says, nudging me, a smile on her lips. Relief floods me. If it's things like History, I can just read to catch up.

"Thank you," I say, blushing. My cheeks are now in a permanant state of red.

Jane leads me to a measuring area. Measuring tapes hang from the walls, and a type of sewing machine stands on an iron platform.

"What am I supposed to stand on?" I ask. Jane just gives me a smug look and presses a button, and the hardwood floor slides apart. A stool made of roots forms. A small bridge leads across to where the stool is.

"Here you are, Miss Wiley," Jane waves her hand, and a root slides into my hand and leads me to the stool.

I try my best not to freak out as roots take my measurements and start giving them to Jane by taking up a quill and jotting down notes on a small pad of paper. Jane sits herself at the iron platform, which holds her sewing machine. She begins sewing, her movements so fast I can barely track them with my eyes.

"This darling, is why Jane Quicksilk is the best seamstress in all of Zilliad," Harlyn says to me as Jane makes quick work of my uniforms.

We leave the shop with five uniforms. All in different cuts but with the same bold ruby color. Some are pants and tunics and others are skirts and frilly shirts. We also purchase two pairs of sturdy brown boots.

"How did you like that?" Harlyn asks, beaming at me.

"It was definitely an experience." I still feel where some roots playfully tickled me.

Blaze laughs.

"You're going to enjoy Tethoris," Harlyn says, grinning.

"Am I going to be assaulted by roots?"

"We'll see." Harlyn grins at my pale cheeks.

Tethoris slides into focus. Simple cottages with warm light pouring from their windows are more modest than those in Gildalynn. Many people are dressed in light browns, but they all wear gleaming smiles that Gildalynn was missing. This seems like a place that I can relate to more. Where people aren't used to having everything all the time and wear plainer colors and live simpler lives.

We follow a sign that says Ruby Road. Window boxes overflow with colorful flowers. Ice sculptures that have more detail than I have ever seen in ice, sparkle in the starlight. Fountains overflow with water, giving the air a light, tinkling noise. All of the shops along the road have a trademark ruby on their door.

Our next stop is a bookstore. The wooden building tips slightly, as if all of the knowledge it holds is making it bend over. Two lanterns hang beside the double doors. A wooden sign hangs above the doors: *Sulkrie's Stories.*

"Who's Sulkrie?" I ask, embracing the smell of books as we step into the dimly lit building. Books line the walls, shelves upon shelves reach up to the ceiling twenty feet above us. A round skylight filters in the evening light.

"The owner," Blaze says.

"Sulkrie!" A man, tall and thin, steps into the room from a door in the back.

"Ah, hello, Hallawells."

His voice is calm and slow, like it's swimming through all the words bouncing around in his head. His eyes fall on me, as I stand awkwardly behind Harlyn and Blaze.

"And addition." He peers at me through warm dark brown eyes. Eyes that hold an abundance of knowledge.

"This is Muriel Wiley, our new addition to the family," Harlyn says.

Sulkrie nods at me, smiling widely. "How can I assist you?" He starts skimming his shelves, which hold books that vary in size, shape, and color.

Harlyn pulls a list from her pocket and hands it to Sulkrie. "Astronomy and Planetary Science, Water bending, Irradiation Bending, Irradiation Bending Science, How to Train Your Dragon, Zilliad History...They still teach history in level three? Pfft."

"My classes use Bender instead of Flecte?" I ask. Everything I have encountered in Zilliad has used Flecte.

"Yes," Harlyn says, slightly distracted. "When you are learning to bend and control the elements they use Bender, Flecte is what we are called."

"Oh, okay," I say, even though nothing she said makes sense.

He mumbles to himself as he scans the shelves. He comes away with a pile of books stacked in his arms. We walk up to the desk, and Harlyn pulls out a little bag of silver coins.

"That'll be six novas," Sulkrie says. Harlyn places six shining coins in his hand. They have a sun imprinted on them and are about the size of my thumb pad.

"You really don't have to do that," I say, blushing. I hated it when they paid for my uniforms. And now they are paying for my books.

"It is no trouble darling," Harlyn says. "We'll go to the Aumary tomorrow to get some of your money out."

"I have money?" Blaze and Harlyn glance nervously at one another. Then turn back to me, nervous smiles plastered on their faces.

"Yes."

They don't provide anything else. I raise an eyebrow but try to shrug it off. I can't be worrying about things that have not happened yet.

This day has been too long already. I have to get used to this world. And maybe read the entire history book tonight just so I don't sound brainless tomorrow.

"Should we go to Nat's?" Blaze asks, grinning.

"Oh, yes." Harlyn takes my hands and tugs me out of the door. "You are going to love her!"

"Apparently I love a lot of things," I mumble under my breath.

They lead me off Ruby Road and through some twisting alleys and along some bridges. Happy families are eating dinner in well-lit cottages. The scent of blooming flowers wafts into my nostrils.

Some children play outside, games that I have never seen before. For one, their parents form disk-light things with their hands and they toss multiple disks back and forth to each other while trying to reach the end of the street.

"What's that?" I ask, trying not to giggle as a kid throws a ball of mud at another.

"Oh, they're playing Disker, one of the sports that we have around here." Blaze turns to me, excited. "Maybe once you get settled at Ravenscroft you could play some sports?"

I nod obligingly for him, but really, just going to Ravenscroft right now terrifies me. What will everyone think of me? Will it be the same as my last school? Will I be the odd one out again?

We cross another bridge and Harlyn points out a shop that glows with warm lamplight. Two wide windows spill laughter and a cinnamon smell into the street. I can make out the word *Nat's* right above the wide wooden door. Harlyn pushes through, and a bell tinkles overhead. Groups of people are dining or just having a cup of tea.

"Are you feeling hungry, sweetie?" Harlyn asks, leading me to an oaken table. "Oh, and try not to stare when Nat comes."

"Why?" I ask, my curiosity piqued.

Blaze just laughs. What is with these people and mysteries? Sitting down, Harlyn waves at a plump wrinkly woman. Her eyes are almost hidden beneath her wrinkles. Is this what I was going to look like when I turn two thousand?

"Nat is one of our special human guests, which also means she is very old. She came from the Corona Ages."

"I'm quite ancient," Nat says, in a crackly voice. I let out a nervous laugh.

"So, you know what the human world is like?" I ask, scooting forward in my chair.

"I do indeed. It isn't a place that is as joyful and safe as this one. Also, the food is better here." She pats my hand. "So, what can I get you?"

I glance at Harlyn, and she shrugs. "Go for it."

I pick up the menu and read off five different random things that I have never heard about before. And I avoid anything that has meat or potatoes in it. I've had enough of those for the rest of my life.

Harlyn and Blaze order as well, and I start leafing through *How to Train Your Dragon*. It's actually quite interesting, not that I would ever want to have, or ride, a dragon.

The serenity is ruptured when three armed men and women dressed in blue and red stomp in, heading straight for Blaze.

"Your Reverence," a man says, bowing his head. The armed people clasp a clenched fist over their right shoulder. Their armor is made of silver, and it bends when they move. It is plated down their arms and legs and across their torso. Tall black boots go up to their knees, and long blue and red cloaks are clasped with a fist clip over their right shoulder.

The one with a red cloak speaks first. "There has been a Dark Monster attack on the West Shore. Your presence is requested."

Blaze glances nervously at Harlyn and me and then nods to the soldiers.

"Be safe," Harlyn says, and clutches her chest, as if in pain.

"Please don't worry too much, love, I'll be fine."

He kisses her cheek and ruffles my hair, which I didn't expect. At all. The touch makes tears spring to my eyes. It was the fatherly touch I hadn't known I was missing. Suddenly, I wish he wouldn't go and fight the Dark Monster. Whatever that is.

They leave, the soldiers' cloaks swishing. A million questions swim through my head. Harlyn looks so sickly, her face has gone pale. What is a Dark Monster? And what is a Reverence? And I really want that silver armor.

We eat in silence, but it doesn't bother me. The food is amazing. Exotic fruits and soups filled with delicious vegetables. Dessert comes, a tiny cake that is dark brown with swirls of red. It is served on a delicate silver platter.

I have never been this full in my life. I sigh contentedly. Harlyn doesn't look as pleased. Her fingers are twitching and she has barely touched her food

"Blaze is going to be okay," I say, and smile. "He seems like someone who can take care of himself."

Harlyn glances at me and nods, her eyes full of uncertainty.

"Let's go home," is all she says in response. In no time at all, Hearthstone towers over us, its shape cut out of the stars behind it.

"Before we head in for the night," I cut in, as Harlyn is about to open the door. She glances back at me, eyes weary.

"Yes?"

I fiddle with my dress. "There were some things I didn't understand that those guards said."

Harlyn nods, encouraging me to go on. But a look in her eyes tells me she isn't up for it, for the questions that will remind her of whatever her husband is doing. "Never mind, actually. It's kind of late."

I take the bags that are filled with my clothes and books from her and head up to my bedroom alone. It feels so wide and empty without the sun shining through the windows.

Stars are reflected in a little fountain that rests near the wide windows.

I lay my favorite uniform out for the next day and put my books into a ruby-encrusted satchel. Underneath some of my books I find a silver box. Inside I find a ring cuff like the one Honora was wearing. I slip it on the wrist that doesn't have the tattoo and fasten the chain from the ring to the cuff. It flashes gold and a sea green stone appears on the underside of the cuff. I fiddle with it for a moment and find a note tucked in the box.

"A sign of being a Water Flecte is this cuff, take it with you always, it will help protect you. The gem stone shows what your color shall be. It will serve to determine your limits."

I set down the note in the box and walk over to my armchair which sits next to my towering windows. Curling up in an armchair that rests next to the windows, I tap a little orb hanging over me and it comes to life, glowing with a bright light.

Blaze and Harlyn are all I would have ever wanted in parents. But the ache of never being able to see Rolia again stings. The day's events finally catch up to me and tears soak the fabric of the chair as I drift off to sleep.

CHAPTER 15

THE COFFIN TRAIN OF DOOM

A soft hand shakes me awake. It takes me a moment to realize that I am no longer in Ractia.

"Time to head to Ravenscroft," Harlyn whispers softly as I try to blink sleep out of my eyes.

Her words sink in as I stretch. I'm about to go to school. Flecte school. I'm going to be run over, again and again. They're all so powerful and I'm just...not.

"You found your ring cuff, good." She shows me hers. It has a sea blue stone set into it. "I'll leave you to get ready," Harlyn says, a wide smile on her face. "Breakfast is cooking, so don't take too long."

"I won't," I mumble as I slip into the bathroom.

The fabric pattern from the chair is imprinted into my rosy cheek. My braid from yesterday is halfway undone. Let's not even get started on my breath. I kick off my clothes from yesterday, take a shower, and tie back my hair into a loose ponytail.

The uniform I picked out yesterday is sprawled on my desk. I stare at the outfit for a moment, still unsure if this is all real.

The uniform is a black pair of pants made of a soft silk, a white, long-sleeved shirt, and a red vest. *Muriel Wiley: Water Flecte* is stitched in gold into the right shoulder of the vest. I notice that each uniform has my name and ability stitched into the right shoulder. The boots that Harlyn bought for me are made of a velvety brown leather that bends with my foot. I enter the kitchen, and Harlyn's eyes fill with tears when she first sees me.

"Sorry," she says, twisting her long blonde hair. "I just never thought I'd see someone under my care in that uniform."

I smile, but my heart is heavy. Why did fate get to decide that these wonderful people didn't get to enjoy having children of their own?

"I'm here now," I say softly.

I join Blaze at the table. Blaze sits across from me, looking very disheveled. His eyes are heavy and dark. He has multiple scratches down his face. He still manages to read his dragon magazine.

"How was the rest of your er…evening?" I lick my lips and fiddle with the silver buttons on my vest.

Blaze glances up from *Scaly Tails*. "It was good."

"So…what was that thing the people in blue and red said? A Dark Monster?" I sit on my hands so I don't twist them.

Blaze clears his throat and flips to the next page. "Oh, those."

"Are they dangerous?" He's being so infuriating and simple with his answers.

"Incredibly."

I grit my teeth.

"Where do they come from?" I ask.

Blaze raises an eyebrow at me. *Give me a solid answer.*

"The Dark King. He was in power thousands of years ago, really gave the Leader and Estrellas a hard time."

He glances at Harlyn, sharing that infuriating you-can't-know look. But I do know. That was a name mentioned by Rolia. Shadows crowd my vision.

"But he is no longer in power, just sends some of his minions every so often to bother us. He stays on his islands mainly, too afraid to reemerge."

My blood runs cold. He was the king of shadows. The one that is beginning to stalk my dreams. Harlyn and Blaze can't know that I met him. Not yet, anyway.

"Oh." I fidget. "And the guards? And Reverence?"

"The guards are the Reds and Blues, depending on their abilities and skill level. They're under the Captain of the Guard." He sets down his magazine. "'The Reverence' is the class Harlyn and I are in. We help support Zilliad and the Leader. Make sense?"

I nod, happy he finally came out and told me more. Even if some of the things were disturbing. The puzzle holds many pieces, and I'm only beginning to build the border. Harlyn places the food down in front of me, a fruit salad and a drink.

"That's bumble-berry tea, it really warms the bones. And just some fruits from the garden." She clutches her chest as she often does and sits down.

"Thank you."

I eat quickly, excitement and fear filling my stomach. The bumble-berry tea does in fact melt away some of the fears that are cramming into my head. It's warm and sweet in a comforting way. Like it was taken straight out of a flower still bathed in sunlight.

"How're you feeling about school?" Blaze asks, his voice slightly muffled by the muffin in this mouth.

"I'm nervous," I blurt. Going to Ravenscroft was going to be a whole new world for me. This is a whole new world.

Blaze chuckles. "'Course you are, but don't sweat it. You'll have a brilliant time, and if someone is mean to you, I have friends who own dragons."

I find myself smiling at that. "Thanks, Blaze. I'll definitely take you up on that. Great first impression."

Blaze laughs lightly.

My eye catches Harlyn moving away, her hand still clutching her chest. "Blaze…." I glance at him. "Is something wrong with Harlyn?"

"What do you mean?" Blaze asks, setting down his magazine. A roaring dragon shows from its pages.

"The unicorns for therapy, how she clutches her chest sometimes, the grey streaks in her hair…I thought we were…immortal or something."

"Harlyn has always had a heart problem that bothers her sometimes." He pauses, then adds quickly. "But it's nothing for you to worry about."

"Okay. I'm sorry. Thanks for letting me know, though."

"Five minutes 'til we have to be in the Square," Harlyn says, swooping into the room and grabbing my plate, which has hardly been touched.

I sling my satchel over my shoulder.

"You got this, El!" Blaze calls after Harlyn and I as we exit the mansion.

"You're going to be fine, El. You'll see," Harlyn says, and takes my hand, calling for the Square.

"I hope so," I mutter just before I dissolve.

We arrive in a place bustling with teens dressed in different-colored uniforms. Kids, who I realize are Level Ones by the color of their uniforms, hug their parents as they filter into a line that has other kids in the same purple uniforms. I feel like they do but resist the urge to grab onto Harlyn and scream for her to take me back.

"This is the first day for everyone, so nerves are high. Don't worry, you're not alone, You have friends already, and Blaze and I will support you through whatever is to come," Harlyn says, and I follow her to a line of students in the same ruby color that I am wearing. Fear takes a hold of me as Harlyn steps away and gives me a thumbs up.

"You're going to do great! Be brave, Muriel Wiley!" And then she's gone. And I'm left alone in a sea of colors, of people I don't know.

"Hey, Waterbug." A voice says from behind me. The voice is teasing, and I recognize it immediately.

I spin around to find Chase, hands casually slipped in his vest pockets. I almost hug him, so relieved to see his familiar face.

"Chase!" I exclaim, then reign myself in. "Hi."

"Good to see you, too," he says, smiling widely. His sea-blue eyes almost disappear as the skin around his eyes crinkle.

"That uniform looks good on you, in an old lady sort of way."

I give him a shove, but his presence makes me sigh in relief. "Thanks. How are you feeling after fainting and, um, flipping your life upside down?"

"Fantastic, it's been absolutely brilliant."

I raise an eyebrow, convinced he's being sarcastic.

"This world is very cool, though. Gildalynn and Tethoris. And how they organize the classes into colors," he says.

I nod. The world is very well organized, but there is always something deeper.

"What are those things?" Chase's words cut into my train of thought. I look where he is pointing.

Five rows of boxes are built onto a train track-type contraption that is built into the mountain. They're color coded, have numbers on each, and labeled "Amethyst," "Aquamarine," "Ruby," "Emerald," and "Diamond." When roughly thirty kids get piled in, a man flicks his fingers and they start clipping up the mountain towards Ravenscroft.

Ravenscroft itself looks magnificent in the morning light. The different levels go up in the colors the school is organized into. It doesn't seem to be big enough to hold all of the kids piling into the train-like contraptions.

"Do you know where Ri is?" I glance around, but I can't find her anywhere. What a terrible best friend I am.

"No, nor our buddy Ty." Chase taps his chin.

"Well, hopefully we'll find them soon enough, because it's our turn next on the train of doom." I have never been very fond of heights. And climbing into a box that heads straight up a mountain makes me terrified. It's like I'm climbing into my coffin.

"Next!" The man on our platform shouts. I climb a set of stairs with Chase right behind me and enter the door that hangs on silver hinges. There is a stairway right in front of me, leading to another level. I decide to stay on the lower level, not wanting to go any higher than I already am going to go.

I choose a spot on the cushioned bench and lean my head back. Chase chooses the seat beside me. A random girl slides into the seat on the other side of me. She smiles, her glasses slipping down her nose.

"Hi, I'm Rosie Halickle. Are you new here?" Her brown eyes glint with curiosity.

"Um, yes… Is it that obvious?"

She laughs sweetly.

"Kinda? I mean there are only around one hundred and fifty kids in the Ruby Level, and you tend to get to know them all well enough when you've gone to school with them for the last two years."

I nod. Then the car lurches, and I clutch Chase's knee.

He chuckles. "Easy there, Waterbug."

I remove my hand with a flush and close my eyes, not wanting to watch the ground slip by quickly below.

"You're going to want to see this," Rosie says. "Ravenscroft is more magnificent than you'd think from below. And these cars are powered by water, as you could tell by the Water Flecte down below," she says, a prideful air in her voice. "I see you're a Water Flecte too, very cool" She points to my ring cuff.

"Yeah. It is." I twist my B.T. ring. "Oh, I didn't notice that." I glance around the car where other level threes are reading or chatting. I notice a small cart that holds scrolls, pens, snacks, and some books. Last-minute supplies for anyone who is forgetful. It will probably come in handy one day for me.

We creep up the mountain, and the valley below us comes into view, the towns stretching forth, the radiant glow of the green. I notice a golden castle tucked slightly behind a mountain.

"Another castle?" I ask, a bit shocked. Rosie laughs at me, and Chase snorts.

"These Flectes are a bit extravagant," Chase says, his nose scrunched a little.

"No, they aren't. Each castle serves a purpose. Or they wouldn't be there."

"Of course, sorry," Chase says, grinning.

"And you are...?" Rosie asks, eyeing him.

"El's irresistibly handsome bodyguard. Though the position may be opening if she decides to jump out the window of this car." He winks, and Rosie blushes. In fact, I was thinking about it, but decided against it as we begin to approach closer to the castle. The car swerves and levels off, and that's when I realize Ravenscroft is built into the mountain. The castle is only the beginning. There are stairs twisting up and around leading to more rooms and halls that are in different sections according to the level you are in. The cars take us up a track and into a small cave-like area where we all unload. Lanterns light a path of smooth stone as we climb up the stairs and into a stunning room.

"Whoa," I breathe and turn on my heel. There are rubies hanging from delicate chains that are making reflections throughout the room. A huge blown-glass chandelier is tucked into the ceiling. Windows that stretch into the sky show off the entire valley.

"This is the Antechamber. The lockers are down that way." Rosie points to the left.

"Then hopefully, you can find your way around the rest of the castle. I hope to see you in class, El?"

I nod, and she takes off to go find her friends.

"We're bound to get lost," Chase says, sighing dramatically. "But at least our shoes are made of leather so we can eat them."

"You're weird," I grumble.

"El!" a voice shouts, and a small blonde girl shoves towards me.

"Ri," I say with a sigh of relief. She hugs me and then pulls back, checking to see if I'm okay.

"How're you doing?" I ask, glad to see her in one piece.

"Good! I made a friend, or well she found me, and Ty is this way, too."

She leads us through the crowd of people, and eyes follow us. Rosie was right, there aren't too many people in this level. Just enough to make the room crowded. But I don't feel too overwhelmed. My school in Ractia was way more overcrowded.

Ty is standing next to a red-headed girl. She gives me a half smile, holding back. Her blue eyes are guarded.

"This is Neva Warden. Her brother is another person in our Tribe."

"I'm El." I extend my hand, and she shakes it uncertainly. "Where's your brother?"

"Who knows? He isn't very good with new people." Her voice holds an edge. What made this girl so untrusting?

"Oh," I say, trying to not sound disappointed. Of course, we had to have someone who doesn't want to meet us as a part of this team. But didn't Lady Dez say he has always wanted a Tribe?

"I'm Chase, the cool one," Chase says, grinning widely. "Tell your brother he's missing out."

"You can tell him yourself in class when you go to Tribe Training," Neva says, eyeing him suspiciously.

"Neva was going to help us get settled in," Ri says, breaking the silence that was spreading between us.

"That's nice of you," I say, smiling.

Neva just nods.

"Paron Brooks will be welcoming us to a new school year in a minute, then I will help you find your way to class. It can be pretty easy to get lost."

I nod at her.

"I guess we won't have to eat our shoes then," Chase whispers to me.

"What a shame, I was looking forward to that."

Music begins, some kind of fanfare. A lady walks out of a doorway and makes her way to a small platform. She smiles kindly at us and pulls on her red jerkin. The music cuts out.

"Greetings, new Ruby Level students! I am Paron Brooks." She nods at us. "If you need anything come to me. The Ruby Level welcomes you!" She smiles wider. "Just beware, a wild gargoyle got out this morning, so please be careful as you make your way to your classes."

A couple people giggle, but I don't. A loose gargoyle? That's welcoming.

"Also, we would like to welcome Ri Simons, Muriel Wiley, Chase Cutler, and Ty Ramenoff to Zilliad!" A spotlight shines on us, and I decide I want to die. No one says anything or does anything, which is almost worse than just standing in silence.

She leaves, and everyone begins to stare at us, not moving.

"Yes, we're new and amazing! But that doesn't mean we like all this attention! Move along!" Chase says, and I almost hug him. Twice already he's saved me today.

Everyone moves away, whispering among themselves.

"This way," Neva says, and we follow her down the hallway after the crowd, deeper into the halls of Ravenscroft.

CHAPTER 16

WELCOME TO RAVENSCROFT

We follow Neva into another large chamber that is filled with lockers. Stairs lead to a second level, which holds more lockers.

Neva pulls out a list from her pocket. "Paron Brooks gave this to me when she appointed me to show you around." So she was told to take us? That may be why she doesn't seem like she wants to be here.

"Lockers one twenty through one twenty-five." Following Neva past a sparkling fountain in the center of the room, we come to five metal lockers. There are no handles or lock codes, just a small hole right at eye level.

"How do I open this…?" I ask, feeling embarrassed. Ri, Chase, and Ty look equally puzzled.

"Lean in and open your eyes really wide. They take a retina scan to open," Neva explains and stands beside me, waiting. I open my eyes as widely as I can, and a green light flashes over them, enabling the ruby red locker to swing open. My eyes water.

"You'll get used to it," Neva mutters, then moves to help the others. Inside the locker, a scroll tied with a red ribbon sits on the top shelf, as well as a black shirt and pants. Black boots sit beside them.

"Those are your self-defense uniforms," Neva says, from beside Ri.

I nod, slightly surprised about having Self-Defense class. I hadn't known about that. There's a little note attached to the string tying up the scroll. It reads:

Keep this with you at all times.

I grab the scroll and open it up:

You will be with the rest of the Ruby segment for all your classes, except Waterbending and Tribal Training.

Monday: 9:30 Arrival, 10:00 Irradiation Bending, 12:00 Lunch, 1:00 Waterbending, 3:00 Departure

Tuesday: 9:30 Arrival, 10:00 Self-Defense, 12:00 Lunch, 1:00 Tribal Training, 3:00 Departure

Wednesday: 9:30 Arrival, 10:00 Irradiation Bending Science, 12:00 Lunch, 1:00 Waterbending, 3:00 Departure

Thursday: 9:30 Arrival, 10:00 Self-defense, 12:00 Lunch, 1:00 Tribal Training, 3:00 Departure

Friday: 9:30 Arrival, 10:00 Irradiation Bending, 12:00 Lunch, 1:00 Waterbending, 3:00 Departure

Saturday: 9:30 Arrival, 10:00 Zilliad History, 12:00 Lunch, 1:00 Tribal Training, 3:00 Departure

Tuesday and Thursday Evenings: 9:00 Astronomy and Planetary Science will be held at the Star Tower.

Your teachers
Zilliad History: Pundit Quinn
Waterbending: Pundit Alora
Self Defense: Pundit Clay
Tribal Training: Pundit Lee
Irradiation Bending Science: Pundit Lee
Irradiation Bending: Pundit Cora
Astronomy and Planetary Science: Pundit Astra
Head of Ruby Level: Paron Brooks

I groan inwardly. Five days of school was already enough. But six? But Flecte school only has two subjects a day, besides the special days that have Astronomy and Planetary Science, which I'm excited to start.

"Ri and I have the same class, so we'll be heading there. Good luck!" Neva says, slinging an arm around Ri and leading her off. Ri casts me a hopeless look, but lets herself get steered away. Chase and Ty have disappeared as well, and I am utterly alone. And very lost.

I unload some of my books, only taking the ones I need for Irradiation Bending and Tribe Training, which are my subjects for the day. How I'm going to find where they are, beats me. The back of my schedule reads where the classes take place, but the instructions are very vague.

Sighing, I slip my books into my bag and spin around, starting to walk, but I slam into someone rushing through the room. We go sprawling across the floor, books and legs going everywhere.

"Ow," someone groans. I pick myself up and turn around to find a small blonde girl rubbing her knee.

"I'm so sorry, are you all right?" I ask, hurrying over to her and falling to my knees in front of her. I begin grabbing some of her books, which have been splayed all over the floor. She glances up at me and I am startled by her ice-blue eyes. Her heart-shaped lips turn into a frown.

"Yeah, I'm fine," she mutters, and I help her to her feet, collecting the rest of her books and settling them into her arms.

"Sorry, again."

"It's really—hey! You're the new girl, aren't you?" A bright smile lights up her face.

"Oh, um, yeah." I blush under all of the eyes turned our way.

"I'm Ash." She smiles sheepishly, like she's ashamed of her outburst. I hide a laugh.

"Muriel." I readjust the satchel on my shoulders, scanning above the crowd trying to find my friends. Ash takes her books from me, and smiles.

"Since it's your first day, would you like me to help you find your way to class?" she asks.

"I look that lost?" I ask, but grin.

"Yeah," she switches to a whisper. "I got lucky. You seem cool, I mean, you're a Water Flecte, like, lucky." She gestures to the words on my shoulder.

"Oh, yeah." I twist my fingers together and she bumps my arm playfully.

"Don't be so sullen, this is a good thing. I get to be friends with the new girl." Her smile is contagious.

I feel a grin twist my lips up. "Friends?" I ask. Friends have never been an easy thing for me. The fact that she ran into me is probably a good thing. Or else I would probably never have spoken with her. I nod and smile, "Yeah, friends."

Ash leads me to class, which we arrive at after a million twists and turns. We even go on the transport that we took up here, again.

"How do you know how to get everywhere? This level should be new to you too." I voice my thoughts aloud as Ash leads me through what feels like hundreds of halls.

"We had a tour the other day. They showed us around." She glances back at me. "Guess you weren't here for that."

"Oh, yeah."

We enter a light-filled classroom. A huge glass desk stands at the front of the wide room. Colorful tapestries hang behind it showing different dimensions of where light comes from.

Ash and I find seats towards the back, and I slump into my seat, glad to be sitting. Ash sits behind me, grinning.

"Hey, Ash," a boy says from the desk across from us. He grins, but Ash's face goes from pleasant to insanely annoyed in a second.

"*Collin Evans*," she growls. I don't see why she's annoyed. He doesn't seem mean. His lopsided grin is anything but a sneer.

He is tall, long legs sticking out awkwardly from beneath his desk. He has a giant pile of books in front of him, all with bookmarks stuck in them. I do read, but not like that.

"I see you've made friends with the new girl," He glances at me, wide brown eyes curious. "Very cool."

I laugh nervously. "Hi," I manage.

"I'm Collin, the smartest kid in this level." He lowers his voice to a whisper, leaning towards me. "Maybe even this school."

"Muriel, or El. It's nice to meet you." I try not to giggle as Ash lowers herself in her seat, brooding.

"If you ever need anything, feel free to hit me up with any questions, 'cause I got all of 'em."

I nod. "I may have to take you up on that."

Ash mutters something behind me which sounds like, "Dear light, no."

I notice Chase and Ty are sitting further towards the back of the class, and Ri and Neva are further off to the right. Why they ditched me when I was in the same class as them makes no sense to me. The entire level is here as well. I count five rows of thirty desks. This is the largest classroom I have ever been in, and they must all be like this. At least it makes it easier on the teachers, or harder. How they manage to keep every student under control, beats me. One hundred and fifty students in one classroom must be chaotic.

But that's when I meet Pundit Cora. She is tall and stern faced. Her dark hair is pulled back sharply into a bun. Her red dress looks like it's made up of angles all sharp and pointed. Her piercing gaze seems to watch all of us at once. Everything about her is sharp.

"Good morning, pupils," her voice echoes about the room. Slicing. Cold. Everyone goes silent.

"We will be starting from the beginning, since you have not done this before. Turn in your Irradiation Bending textbooks to page, well, one."

Hundreds of hands reach into their satchels and retrieve their books. I flip to the page instructed and wait.

"Bending of the light…." and she trails off into a lengthy lecture about the properties of pulling light from this dimension and others.

None of it makes sense. I glance back at Ash and she shrugs. Collin is writing everything down, flipping through his pile of books, and nodding right along with her.

I can barely spot my friends over the heads of the other students.

"Now practice what I have said," she says, and begins sweeping around the room, going from desk to desk.

I hold out my hand, just like she had when giving an example, and focus on the tips, where light is streaming through them with every pulse of my heart. I feel a prick, like something is hovering outside of my control. I wrap my consciousness around it and a flicker of light flashes between my fingertips.

"Very good, Muriel Wiley," a cold voice says from behind me. I jump and whip around.

Pundit Cora is hovering over me, eyes cold.

"T-thanks," I mutter.

She nods her head and moves on to torture another group of students.

"Light, Muriel," Ash breathes behind me. "You just survived the witch of the Ruby Level."

Collin looks at me with jealousy, and I can't help but smile.

After what feels like ages, Pundit Cora dismisses us. I get carried away by the crowd as they all make it towards the Hall of Eatery, as it's called on the back of my schedule. To get there we have to take the transport carts, which I learn are called Levonos. I'm crammed between two kids that I don't know as the Levonos makes its way down to the main section of the Ruby Level, where the Antechamber is located.

Rosie finds me, and I walk with her. She chats endlessly about the first lesson with Pundit Cora. Two of her friends eye me curiously. But I'm glad for their presence. I hate being alone here.

"I'll catch you later, El," Rosie says and parts off. I stand in the entrance looking out over the kids gathered at tables, others grabbing lunches from a line.

I file into line, hoping to catch sight of anyone who is familiar, even Collin. But Ash finds me first, and she's standing with Ri and Neva.

"There you are!" Ash says, and sidles into line with me, grinning at the kid she had just cut. He scowls but goes back to talking with his friend.

"I met your friends," she says, gesturing to Neva and Ri.

"Oh?" I grin at Ri, who smiles back. "Let's get food, I'm starving."

Ty and Chase join the rest of us, and we eat, nerves still high from all of the new information.

"Did anyone else have tingly fingers during class?" Chase asks, a pink fruit in one hand. He's wiggling the fingers of his other hand like they're going to start tingling again.

"Yes," I say, laughing.

"I'm kind of used to it," Ash says, and everyone looks at her eyes wide. She smiles. "I've been training because I play a Flecte sport that requires my ability."

"That's really cool," Ty says, and they jump into a conversation about Flecte sports. I only half listen, toying with my food.

"You ready to meet my brother?" Neva asks, looking more excited to be around us than this morning.

I just nod, and continue playing with my food. But that's exactly what I am worried about. What if he hates us? What if we have to get someone new in our group because of it? So many things can go wrong.

And just because I'm in school, making friends and getting homework, doesn't mean I'm not a Protector. I still have a dangerous destiny that's looming towards me. Who knows when I'll have to leave on a top secret mission. Maybe I won't come back one day. I'm not a normal girl, even in this world where I feel myself finally belonging.

My nerves ball themselves into a tight circle in my stomach, and I can't get them to unwind, no matter how many times I try.

The fact that Devlyn didn't come see us during lunch makes me feel like he doesn't want to meet us at all.

We wave goodbye to Ash and Neva and make our way to the Tribe Training room, which is just down the hallway from the Antechamber, so it isn't too hard to find.

Chase pushes through the door we were instructed to enter, and we find a lady and a tall, dark-haired boy sitting in chairs that are gathered in a circle. Four are empty.

But what really strikes me is how good-looking the boy is. His storm-grey eyes spark as they settle on us, and he raises an eyebrow in a bored way. They stand and come towards us.

"Welcome, pupils. I hope you had a good first day of school. Consider today as a day to meet each other before we get into anything serious," Pundit Lee instructs, getting to her feet to greet us. She kisses us all on the cheeks, twice. I hope I don't look as startled as I feel.

"It's the formal way of greeting, I'm Devlyn," he says, letting a tiny smile through, his dark skin flushing slightly. Guess I do look as flustered as I feel. I nod and he extends one of his hands to me.

I shake it. "Muriel."

He introduces himself to the rest of my friends. Once he's done, Pundit Lee leads us to the chairs. And our first Tribe Training commences.

CHAPTER 17

FLOATING ON A SHIMMERING SEA

"How was your first day of school?" Harlyn asks when I arrive back to the Hallawell mansion.

"It was tiring, really tiring. I met my whole level at lunch, learned that I can manipulate light, then had to pour out my biggest secrets to my tribe. Yet the sad thing was, the biggest secret was that I slept with a stuffed animal until I was five, and that I stole apples from time to time."

Harlyn laughs. "Wow, that's *terrifying*. How do some Lemon Bursts sound?"

"Well, those sound yummy, so yes," I say, as I slouch into the kitchen after her. I fall into a chair, throwing my satchel down. Harlyn plops down beside me, a platter of Lemon Bursts in hand. She settles the platter before me and I restrain myself from stuffing my face.

"Where's Blaze?" I ask between bites. I think I could eat these Lemon Bursts all day.

"He's at some meeting for the Leader, nothing too dangerous," she says, smiling. "Did you get any homework?" She seems so excited to talk about how my first day of school went. So I tell her everything, the classes, the teachers, and the kids who were nice.

"Pundit Cora is downright maniacal. She assigned me a three-page essay just on the feeling I got when I first felt the light. How am I supposed to do that?" Reaching for another Lemon Burst, my fingers close around nothing but air. I had eaten all of them. Muttering under my breath, I slouch lower in my chair.

"I'm sure you'll be fine. You are an intelligent, clever, young lady," She ruffles my hair and takes the platter. I blush from the compliment. "Cheer up, buttercup."

I smile. "How're you feeling?" I ask.

Harlyn pales and clutches her chest. "I-I'm fine. Nothing to worry about," she says and forces a smile. I nod, but am not convinced. Harlyn shuffles her feet so I decide to change the subject.

"Do you think I could read something from the library?"

"Of course, darling. Blaze and I want you to feel at home here." She reaches to brush some hair off my cheek but retracts her hand, like touching me might burn her.

I try not to feel hurt as I leave the room.

I scan the tall shelves in the library, scaling ladders until I find what I'm looking for. *The Land of Light: Estrella*. Once I find it, I settle down in the library on a plush chair, the thick book in my hands. Gold stars are sprinkled all over the leather.

The fireplace crackles and sparks disappear into the chimney as I open the heavy cover. It is a history book that's on my list for Zilliad History, so I am glad to find it here. I thought I might have to go to the library in Tethoris.

I really don't want to find my way around another place any time soon. Ravenscroft was way more complicated to manage than I expected. And that was already with help.

I become fully engrossed in the book. It's written from the point of view of a young woman with the initials L.D. She has a special set of unique powers and appears to be royalty before the Leaders were a thing. There's a line that doesn't make sense to me. My head tries to wrap around what I am reading again and again, but it doesn't make sense.

"Harlyn?" I call. Maybe she'll have the answers to my questions. She hurries in, a worry line etched between her brows. "What are the other Flectes like? The Shadow Flectes?"

Harlyn pales and sits down across from me, like her knees can't support her weight anymore. She puts a hand to her forehead and squeezes her eyes shut. When she opens them, fear and worry radiate from her grey-blue eyes.

"This is something we do not discuss, Muriel," Harlyn warns me. "Something our society wants to forget. Something we are ashamed of. I will tell you now so you do not go around talking and asking questions about this."

I scoot forward in my seat, curiosity burning inside of me.

Harlyn leans back, and begins, "There used to be another piece of this island. Another group of people who worked and lived among the Light Flectes. They were called Shadow Flectes. We ended up fighting and splitting the islands apart, spreading a wide gap between the two islands. There has been tension and hatred between the two ever since. Bringing the two groups together again has been discussed. But there would be so much pain. Light and darkness are not supposed to be together."

"What if we should come back together?" I ask, twisting my fingers.

"El, it may seem like a good idea, but the pain from it," she closes her eyes. "We cannot do that again."

"Why would there be pain if we were working towards peace?"

Harlyn sighs. "I fear the only way to get them to listen would be through war."

"Oh…." I glance down at my fingers and find that they are shaking. "I'm sorry I asked you so many questions."

"It's all right, El, but do not worry about it too much. There are some things that don't deserve to take our mental space."

"What happened to my blood parents? Did they not want me or something?" I ask, almost in a whisper. Harlyn takes my hands, tracing a line on the inside of my palms.

"They died a long time ago, Muriel. They loved you very much, though, you were not forgotten. Or unwanted. But it is best not to dig them out of their grave." She pats my leg and rustles away.

They loved me, cared for me. But I had never known them. Never felt their love. But it still feels like losing a piece of me all over again. If they were alive, maybe I could have seen them. But Harlyn's words extinguished any hope I had of meeting them.

Harlyn's earlier words echo around my head. The words she had said about the Shadow and Light Flectes.

This is something I can look into. What if I had been meant to bring us together again? Maybe me being brought up with humans opened up my perspective on the fact that hatred is not the way. The Flectes need peace.

One thing I do know is that I am not going to drop this. I will bring peace.

I continue to read until darkness falls over the room. I hear the front door open and stick the bookmark into the wrinkled pages. I go into the kitchen and Blaze is there, sitting with his dragon magazine, *Scaly Tails*, again. How he got there so fast surprises me.

"Hey, Blaze," I say and sit down across from him. He sets down his magazine and smiles.

"Hello, El. How was school?"

I tell him the same thing I told Harlyn and he chuckles.

"The first day of school is never fun, but tomorrow will be better. I promise. Harlyn's out on assignment, but she will be back later. She left dinner over there on the counter." He points to a platter heaped with food. I hadn't even realized that Harlyn had left.

"Thanks. What're you reading?" I go over and grab the food, which appears to be leftovers from last night. It's fine with me. I'd eat this food over and over again if I had to.

"Oh, this is *Scaly Tails*."

I already knew that from the cover, but I don't really know what to talk about. "You seem to love it," I comment, and he smiles at me, his eyes twinkling.

"Indeed, I do. Harlyn says I'm addicted to it, and I might very well be."

I laugh.

"Muriel, I have a question. And it's totally up to you to answer."

I nod, allowing him to continue.

"How would you feel about Harlyn and I adopting you?"

I make myself not drop my fork. This question had been coming. But am I worthy of them?

"I would love that," I tell him honestly.

He smiles at me and warmth courses through my veins. I would be happy with them, loved even.

I finish my dinner in silence, thoughts stampeding through my mind. Trying not to be awkward, I wish Blaze a goodnight, and go upstairs to do my homework.

Ash and Chase wait for me at the Levonos. Ri is nowhere to be found, but Chase tells me she rode up with Neva. I try not to feel betrayed. I know Ri is just making new friends. But I can't help but feel hurt.

Ravenscroft begins to make a little more sense. Ash and Chase enter with me into the Antechamber. We grab our Self-Defense outfits then head for the locker rooms.

Our teacher for Self-Defense, Pundit Clay, is a beefy man with arms as big around as tree trunks. When he asks for us to fight in hand-to-hand combat, he chooses me to show some of the moves we will be using.

Standing on a mat facing him, I raise my hands before my face, balling them into fists. Pundit Clay swipes my feet from underneath me in two seconds then goes to punch my face. I dodge clumsily, stumbling over my own feet and crashing to the ground. I pick myself up, stars dancing before my eyes.

He growls at me, "Lesson one, learn to control where your body goes."

With every opponent I face, I get knocked to the ground over and over again. My arms and legs don't seem to want to work together to defend me in any way. I'm so covered in bruises by the end that I can barely move.

At lunch Ash sets a red drink that looks like a slushy in front of my plate of food. "Drink this, it'll help. I promise."

I down it in one gulp and immediately my aches seem to melt away. "What is this stuff?" I ask, my head spinning.

"A mixture my Plant Flecte friend makes, really good, right?"

"Yeah, it is." I say grinning widely at her. "I think I'm going to need this more often if my skills remain the same."

"She's right about that," Chase mumbles.

I head to my Waterbending session all alone. Nervousness twisting my stomach. People have told me that Pundit Alora is insanely talented, which only adds to my nerves.

I follow the map of the school till I come to the correct door. I can't tell if I should knock or just go in. I go for a knock.

An elegant lady opens the door. A sea-blue dress swishes around her, making it look like she is floating on a shimmering sea.

"Welcome, Muriel Wiley." Her voice is as smooth as a rippling brook.

"I-I'm excited to get started, Pundit Alora," I say, bowing my head.

She smiles brightly and stands aside, guiding me inside. Two chairs sit in the middle facing each other. Water cascades down all of the walls. It then goes from there and up, circling about the room where it finishes its cycle in a small basin inlaid into the wall. Shapes take place and dance around, leaping and splashing playfully.

"Sit, child. There is much to talk about."

I take one of the silver chairs, which is surprisingly comfortable. The metal molds into my shape. Pundit Alora sits across from me and grabs my hands.

I force myself not to pull away. She closes her eyes. Her eyelashes glitter with gold flecks.

After a couple uncomfortable minutes, she opens her eyes. "Great power is within you, my child. Now I can sense why I was called to teach you."

She releases my hands and smiles at me. The fact that she keeps calling me "child" unsettles me. And she was "called" for me? I wonder who called her and why.

"You will be a great Water Flecte. It is in your blood."

"How can you sense that?" I ask. *In my blood*. Queue the ominous flutters.

"The water inside of you calls to me, telling me things that you are unable to sense."

"Oh. That's…cool." I can't tell how I feel about any of this.

She's talking in riddles. I feel like an awkward rhinoceros.

"Now we must get to your lesson. Today you will begin to learn the basics of finding and calling on the water that is within you."

I nod and she stands. She closes her eyes and spreads her hands. Water pours from her fingers. It comes from within her. She smiles, like the water is an old friend coming to say hello. The water shapes into a large bird that takes flight, swooping around the room, reaching for the sunlight outside. My jaw drops. This lady is seriously powerful.

"Now it is your turn, my child." She gestures for me to join her. "It is within you, call on it."

I close my eyes just as Pundit Alora had done and try not to feel ridiculous. But then I feel it, a tickle on my palms, a tug in my stomach. A need fills my stomach and grows. I pop open my eyes and see my fingertips dripping. It looks like when the water runs down your arms and goes off your fingertips in the shower.

I glance at Pundit Alora, who is watching with calm eyes, but I am totally terrified. I had only ever called on the water around me, not the water within me.

"Ask it for more," she whispers, acting oblivious to my fear.

I close my eyes and pour my concentration on the power deep inside me. Water streams out of my fingers in a torrent. It splatters on the ground, wetting my boots and sinking into my socks.

"Ask it to do something," she commands, waving her hands and forming a unicorn, which gallops around me. It scatters my thoughts with the water it leaves behind. I wave my hands as well and end up making a clumsy blob of water.

"Wonderful. Now that is enough for today. You learned how to call it from within. Friday we will work on control. Now, let us sit and talk about what you can do."

~

At the end of class, I file into the auditorium, my boots slogging from the water, shoulders slouching. I call the water out of them and ask it to go back in through my fingers. It doesn't work. Or listen. So I end up throwing it in the fountain in the center of the room.

The rest of my session with Pundit Alora had been about what I can do with my power, and the danger of it. Once I become more powerful, the water will call for me, like a craving I can't resist. She explained that I need to learn how to control the urges to maintain moderation. It creeped me out how powerful Water Flectes can be. The fact I could drown someone with a snap of my fingers is terrifying. I'm not ready for any of this. Any of this power and responsibility. Everything is going too quickly.

Shifting through my homework, I feel a tap on my shoulder and turn around to find Ash, dressed in an ice-blue body suit thing. She looks like an icicle superhero.

"Umm…." I trail off, she laughs.

"I'm here to invite you to my race." She twists her ponytail around in her finger.

"Race?" I ask. That would probably explain the suit, and the number one written in bright white on the back of her suit.

"Yeah, it is a sport for Ice Flectes. We race on the ocean to get to a certain point. It is called Floe Racing. They're only scheduled when there's a storm."

"A storm?" I ask. Ash didn't appear to me like a daredevil, but I'm learning new things every day. "That sounds dangerous."

"It is, but it's fun, as well."

"Sure, but I'd better ask Harlyn and Blaze." I pull out my Conveyer, which Harlyn had given me this morning. It's basically a smartphone, except it is made out of crystal and is powered by the sun. It's about as thin as paper though, and I'm terrified if I tap it too hard it'll shatter.

"She said yes. What time is it at? I think I'll probably change beforehand." Ash grins at me.

"Great. It starts at sundown, but we'll make it back in time for Astronomy and Planetary Science. I'll see you there." She winks and marches away.

CHAPTER 18

HEY, TROUBLE

Ri and I travel smoothly out to silver stands in small boats that seemed unfazed by the slashing water from the torrential downpour. I'm wearing a giant green parka, which now feels pointless because the water isn't even touching me.

Ri and I get to the stands, which are packed with people holding banners and flags in different shades of blue. Team symbols flap in the wind. Giant glowing balls of light, which float over the water, are not being dimmed by the slashing rain. The waves are mountainous but they don't touch our stands. It's probably more Water Flecte magic.

Pushing our way up sleek silver steps we make it to the top where Ri and I find seats.

The racetrack stretches about three hundred yards and is lit up from globes under and over the water. It begins on a beach and then finishes on a small island. These Floe Races seem super dangerous to me. But maybe not. I'm new here and afterall, the Flectes seem to like a little danger every so often.

"Hey, Trouble," a voice I recognise says from behind me.

I jump, turning around to find Chase, Ty, and Devlyn, their cheeks painted in the color of Ash's team color.

"Another nickname?"

"Why not?" Chase asks, smirking. He pulls my braid. "Nice parka." I blush and roll my eyes. "Now don't go rolling those pretty green eyes at me, Waterbug. We wouldn't want them getting lost in your head."

"Thanks for the advice." I pull water from all around me and splash him in the face with a little bubble.

"I see you've learned to use your power. I'd use mine on you, but since it is *illegal* to use it, I better not. Wouldn't want to get kicked out as I've only just arrived."

"That *would* be a shame."

"It would. Wouldn't it?" He grins at me, and I feel a smile tugging at the corners of my mouth. He might be annoying at times, but he does know how to make me smile.

A horn blasts through the air, pulling my attention to where the dome of light stands on the beach. Ten figures, all in tight bodysuits, stand in a line, ready to take off at the next blow of the horn. I spot Ash, standing at the far end, her bright blue suit standing out boldly against the grey sand.

A wave fifty feet high crashes against the barriers of the stands.

That girl is brave.

"Is she going to be all right?" I ask no one in particular.

"Ash has been doing this her whole life, don't worry about her," Devlyn assures me.

I invited him. Chase's voice says inside my head. *I thought it would be good for us to hang out with him. Though we got lucky that you're here, too. So now the whole family can hang out!*

I nod at him, mouthing the words *thank you.*

"Okay," I respond to Devlyn. "Thanks."

He smiles widely and I grin back. Ri elbows me and grins, the kind of grin that makes my cheeks flame.

A second horn blasts through the air whipping me from my thoughts. Blasts of ice shoot from the hands of the racers as they begin. They race along the ice until a wave comes along, which is when they dive out of sight into the wall of crashing water, making my breath stop in my throat. They emerge on the other side, but I notice two are missing.

Ash is still going, and she's flying. She moves in a rhythm that can only come after years of practice. Her movements are synchronized. She's a ballerina on ice.

Suddenly a giant wave comes out of nowhere and crashes over her and another boy, who is in the lead. A collective gasp goes up from the crowd, and two medics prepare themselves for a rescue on two silver machines that look like bikes. But two bodies resurface after about a minute. A sigh of relief echoes through the stands.

Ash and the other boy have left everyone else behind, even after their wave incident. The waves are just too large for the other competitors. Two rescue medics have eight racers on the back of their boats.

I am just thinking it can't get any more dangerous, when they start blasting each other with gleaming icicles. My hand goes to my mouth as Ash dives to escape one. She quickly recovers herself and launches one back at the other boy. It grazes his back, leaving a trail of red behind them in the water.

They only have about ten yards left to go. My throat becomes raw with cheering. Everyone had been in intense silence at first, but now we are screaming encouragement and glaring at the others who are cheering for the boy.

Ash sends one last icicle at the boy, who sends one at her at the same time. It scrapes his arm and her leg. But Ash makes a last-minute blast and she skids onto the island seconds before the boy.

I jump to my feet and whoop. A thrill of pride rushes through me. Victory courses through my veins. Medics rush out to the island and tend to Ash and the boy, who had suffered minor injuries during the race.

"Yeah, Ash!" I see Collin jumping up and down, and I feel like laughing.

"That was amazing!" Ri squeals. "I don't think I'll ever do it, but it sure is fun to watch." Ty nods in agreement. "I visited the library today before the race and read about it. It seemed like a really cool thing, but seeing it in person. Just wow."

Ri nods her delicate head. I glance back at Ty, and he smiles at me. I have not checked on him at all, or really spoken with him. I feel slightly ashamed for not checking on him. But at the same time, I've known him for such a short time. I glance around. Chase and Devlyn are deep in conversation, and Ri and Ty are talking animatedly. I've hardly known any of them for very long. But I feel a sense of belonging with them. Maybe everything would be okay.

"Are we allowed to go see her?" I ask Devlyn, breaking the conversation up between Chase and him.

"She'll be brought up here once they've treated her injuries," he explains, and I nod.

Suddenly a commotion on one of the lower bleachers breaks out. Light flashes, and water is shot through the air. Sounds of a fight hits my ears.

"Not again," Devlyn grumbles, breaking through the crowd, running down the stairs. I follow close on his heels, curiosity burning inside of me. A girl with black hair, tipped with purple highlights, blasts a light dagger at a girl who looks very familiar, and who thankfully, blocks the light daggers with another wave.

"Neva! Stop!" Devlyn exclaims, running into the fight. He dodges a blast of water and dives at his sister, knocking her to the hard ground.

"Devlyn!" She says his name like a curse. "*Don't* interrupt!" Neva snarls, her red hair tossed into her face by the wind.

"What have I told you about fighting?" he asks, pulling her to her feet but still keeping a tight grasp on her arm.

Neva rolls her eyes exasperatedly. She glares at the girl she was fighting with, who is glowering back with an equal amount of hate.

"I'll get you someday, Moyra."

The girl, Moyra, scoffs. "Doubtful, Forgotten One."

Neva shudders with rage. Obviously, the insult cuts pretty deep. Moyra is about to rush Neva again but I decide to step in. I grab Moyra's arms.

"Get off me, new girl," she hisses. "You have no right here."

"I have the same amount of rights as you do. And as it appears, you don't have a special ability, since you were merely fighting with light. So, currently, I am above you."

An "ooh" goes up from the crowd that has gathered around the fight. Moyra glowers at me. I don't like using the fact that she doesn't have a special ability over her head, but it had to happen if I was going to protect Neva.

"That is none of your business," she snarls, shaking off my grip.

"It's very much my business, since you were fighting and insulting my friend."

Moyra arches a thin eyebrow, her high cheekbones creating shadows on her face."You're friends with the Forgotten One?" She laughs. A high and evil thing.

"Yes, now shove off."

Moyra rolls her eyes and stomps away. By then, everyone in the stands is watching. I go over to Neva, ignoring the stares of the surrounding crowd. "You okay?"

"I'm fine." She shakes off her brother and disappears into the staring crowd.

"Why would they call her 'Forgotten One?'" I ask Devlyn.

He looks at me, grey eyes stormy. "Her parents left her, El. That rarely happens here. So it's given a title." He shoves his hands into his pockets, staring after where his sister disappeared.

"Oh."

According to Harlyn, my parents died a long time ago. The pain of them not being here with me is a black hole. But if my parents left me purposefully? That would cut deeper than a knife.

"Should we go after her?" I ask, staring after where Neva's flaming hair had disappeared.

"Naw, she needs to blow some steam off." Devlyn shrugs.

"This happens often?" I ask, noticing that Ash is making her way over to the stands on a boat. Collin is clambering through the crowd to get to her.

"Yes. It just depends if someone sets her off. She gets touchy when it comes to her parents."

"That's understandable." I start in the direction of Ash, but Devlyn grabs my arm.

"Don't say anything about it, okay?"

I nod in agreement. Sharing other people's secrets has never been my thing. Gossip is unnecessary and only used to hurt people.

Ash climbs some stairs and stands on a platform, accepting cheers. A gold medal is placed around her neck in the shape of a snowflake. She makes her way down the platform, and I run and give her a hug. She laughs and hugs me back.

"Congrats," I whisper, and she grins at me. Her quiet confidence is reassuring.

"Thanks, and thanks for coming."

The others come up behind me and congratulate her.

"Are your parents here?" I ask, scanning the crowd. I know if I did something like this Harlyn and Blaze would definitely be here to cheer me on.

"No, they don't really...um do things with me," she says, obviously dodging around the real answer. I raise my eyebrow, but don't ask any more questions. *It's not my business*, I remind myself.

"Oh, I'm sorry," I say, shuffling my feet. She shrugs.

"I'll see you at APS," she says with a grin.

"APS?" I ask.

"Astronomy and Planetary Science, genius."

"Oh, right." I say, with a small giggle.

Ash snorts and we double over laughing, not even sure about what we're laughing about. The laughter feels like a breath of fresh air.

Right then and there, a sense of belonging envelops me. I finally belong somewhere.

CHAPTER 19

THE ROLE OF A PROTECTOR

Planetary Science is held in the same classroom as Irradiation Science class. Our teacher, Pundit Astra, instructs us to chart all of the stars, passing out scrolls and quills. It may be my new favorite class, since it seems so lowkey. I barely feel behind.

Flecte Astronomy is very different from what human Astronomy was. We take the Levonos up to the top of the mountain, where a circular tower stands. It's made of cut crystal, intricately laid out so that all of the stars in the night sky will be reflected into a giant circular pool that lies completely still at the top level.

Pundit Astra talks in her whispery voice and flits around the room in dark clothes as we copy our constellations on a chart. She smiles secretly, like she knows the secrets the stars hold, and we aren't good enough to know them ourselves. Surprisingly, nothing terrible happens to me. I don't think even fate wants to interrupt the quiet pool that rests at the top of the world.

Ty falls in love with the subject, and he is always raising his hand and asking questions in a whispery voice that is almost like Pundit Astra's. It just cracks me up.

~

The days pass in a blissful blur, and before I know it, a month has passed. School falls into a rhythm, and a happy one at that. All of my subjects are going well, except Self-Defense, which just leaves me with bruises and crushed pride every time I'm in class. The other kids have had this class since they were very young, which leaves me with a lot of catching up to do. My friends are catching up faster than I am, and it only serves to hurt my pride even more.

I'm finally learning how to fight in hand-to-hand combat and am moving up to fighting with weapons. The other day, Ri almost sliced my nose off when she was practicing with throwing stars. She is almost as bad as I am in Self-Defense.

On the one day of the weekend when I don't have classes, I spend time with my family. Yes, my family. Harlyn and Blaze have adopted me officially, and I can't tell whether to laugh or cry, or both at the same time. Even though I've done both.

Blaze is teaching me how to throw knives, and he's helping me work on my combat skills. Harlyn helps me with all of my other subjects. Life honestly couldn't be going any better.

I lie on my stomach, writing an essay for Zilliad History, which my teacher Pundit Quinn had assigned, a creaky man with a slow, drawling voice. Suddenly, a knock resounds on my door.

"Come in!" I call, not even looking at who comes in until they clear their throat. I glance up and almost fall off my bed.

"Leader Honora." I hastily scramble off my bed and curtsy.

"Hello, Muriel. I hope you are doing well." It is not a question, it's a statement, so I decide to stay silent and nod.

"I am here to ask you to commence with your first project as a Protector of this land. Everything I am about to tell you is for you and who you trust to go on the journey with you."

I nod my head to show her I understand.

"There has been a great tension in the last few months between us and the Shadow Flectes."

I had almost forgotten a world existed outside of Ravenscroft. The Shadow Flectes, and the Dark King, and the Dark Monsters, and my biological parents. It all comes rushing back to me. Have I really become that complacent?

"They have not struck yet as far as we know. But we are afraid that they might be right under our noses." Honora begins to pace, her long dark hair swishing behind her.

"There are these stones. They hold our world together, and it will take a while to know that they are gone before it is too late. And we are afraid they might have stolen one. Or all of them. I am assigning you to take two other people to make sure the stones are still secure. I will leave you instructions once you have found out who you would like to journey with you."

My head spins with thousands of questions but I focus on who I should bring, determining pros and cons. "I would like to take Harlyn and Ri." They seem the best choices, my best friend, and my adoptive mom. "One moment, sorry." I twist my fingers. She nods. "How are we not going to get pulled back here right away? I thought we couldn't leave the island."

"That is what I was about to discuss."

She pulls a necklace out of her pocket. A golden crown is strung on a delicate cord. Emeralds adorn the tiny peaks of the crown. "This is a Crownpass. Kings and queens of old used to wear them so they could leave whenever they wished. They have a magical spell that allows you to escape the magic of the island that will pull you back. May I?" She holds up the necklace, and I nod, holding up my hair.

"This is the last Crownpass left. Keep it safe and secret."

I nod and tuck it under my shirt. Of course, she had to entrust me with the last Crownpass. Reality comes crashing back to me. I must remember my responsibility. I'm a Protector, not just a silly fifteen-year-old girl who only worries whether her homework is done on time, or if her friend is winning all of her Floe Races.

"Thank you, my Lady. I am honored."

Honora smiles. "Thank you, for being the brave girl we have always dreamed you would one day be."

I wipe tears away, understanding that these are my last moments as a regular teen girl.

I nod my head, not trusting my words.

"I wish you all the luck." She cups my face in her hand and presses a scroll into my fingers before leaving the room.

As soon as the door shuts, I unravel the paper, excitement and fear filling my stomach.

In a dark forest where the water falls. Our hope and peace hide in the halls. Seek them out and assure their safety, then you will regain all things to where they were naturally.

"A riddle? Seriously?" I whisper. Then, I notice a small compass at the bottom made of crystal. Two tigers and the letters "IA" are engraved on the back. I sink onto my bed and sigh.

I knew this was coming, but the fact that it is *actually* happening is even scarier.

"I can do this," I assure myself. And I can. I study the notes and compass, scrunching my eyebrows together. The key has to be in the paper or compass. I hold both up to the light to get a better read on it and gasp. There are longitude and latitude coordinates inscribed on the back:

20.5937° N, 78.9629° E

I close my eyes, bringing up a map of the world from memory. *India*. I have to go to India. But how?

I pull out my Conveyer and type in the longitude and latitude. A small village pops up with pictures of a large tiger statue standing in the courtyard. So that explains the tigers.

But....

It would be easier to go on my own but someone else having my back might be helpful. I fight the urge to chuck the crystal compass across the room. *This is who you are. You're going to have to embrace it eventually.*

I huff and grab a satchel, slipping the compass and note inside. I close my eyes trying to memorize every detail of the picture of the tiger statue and the small village.

I will have to travel there tomorrow.

It is time to take up my role of being a Protector.

CHAPTER 20

IT'S HARD TO SAY NO.

"Harlyn, I need to talk to you," I mutter the next morning. I'd planned all night long what I was going to say, but it all seems to slip away. How can I ask her to do this for me?

"Alright, sweetie. What do you need?" She sets down the platter of muffins that she was baking.

I twist my fingers. My eyes are heavy from so little sleep. "Could you help me with something?" I glance up at her. "Something dangerous?"

"What do you mean?" she asks, a crease forming between her eyebrows.

I give her the whole rundown of what happened with Honora and the stones. And India. And how I've been chosen as one of the Protectors of this world.

"I'm really sorry I've kept this from you, I just didn't know how to tell you."

"Muriel...this is a lot to take in," she says, sitting down. "I will help you, I just wish you would've told me sooner. So I could have helped you."

"You know now. And I'm sorry I didn't tell you sooner. I was just given my first mission last night, it hasn't really been at the forefront of my mind." I feel terrible asking this of her. But she is one of the only people I trust here.

"When do we leave?" she asks, standing up with a finality about her. Like she's determined to be strong.

"After school. I have to ask Ri if she'll help, as well."

"Alright. I will get some stuff ready. Some weapons and such. Everything is going to be fine."

She must be telling herself that. I keep telling myself the same thing. Besides, what could go wrong?

~

My classes are all extra boring today, they seem to be stuck in sludge. Zilliad History drags by at a pace a snail could have beaten. Or at least it feels that way. I try to act normal at lunch, but the fact that I'm going to be leaving in a couple hours for a possibly dangerous mission with my best friend and my adoptive mom makes me sick. Anticipation courses through me, my foot taps a chaotic pace on the floor.

"Are you okay?" Chase whispers to me as we walk back to the Antechamber after Tribe Training. Ty and Ri chatter about how their classes are going. But Devlyn is watching us closely, his grey eyes narrowed.

"I'm fine," I say, staring at the ground.

"You're all pale and you keep twisting your fingers. I'm pretty sure those are signs of not being okay."

He has me there, it's nearly impossible to hide things from him. He notices everything.

"I... well it's complicated." I drag him over to a corner of the hallway. Devlyn scowls at us but keeps walking.

"I've been given my first mission. As a Protector." I give him a rundown of what I was told to do, the Crownpass, and that the world could fall apart if we fail.

"Oh, whoa." He runs his hands through his hair, spiking it in different directions. "Are you going on your own?"

"No, I'm taking Harlyn and Ri." I try not to look at him when I say it. Why am I even talking to him in the first place? I try to walk away but he takes my hands.

"Muriel, take me, please. I've felt so useless. All I've been doing is going to school and then going home to a family that is not my own. And I feel so itchy, like there's something terribly wrong, and I haven't been able to do anything about it. Let me help you, please," he begs.

"Chase, I can't put you in danger like that...."

He doesn't like the slow life? Where we have plenty to eat and friends to hang out with.

"Please, El, I hate sitting around doing nothing. Especially knowing that you're out there, in danger." He traces his thumb over my knuckles. "Please."

Sighing, I pull my hands away and clutch the Crownpass that hangs around my neck. I guess I already told him everything...but the fact that I've only known him for a month makes me want to not let him come or trust him. But he's saved me again and again. Don't I owe it to him? Is it bad that I would rather risk Chase's life than Ri's?

"Okay, we have to go right now."

A smile lights up his face. Not the expression you would expect from someone you just asked to risk their life.

"Thanks, Waterbug," he whispers.

"Anytime," I say. "Let's hope I don't regret it."

CHAPTER 21

THE DANGER ZONE

"That is not Ri," Harlyn observes. I sigh, placing my head in my hands.

"I noticed. He insisted on coming."

Chase stands awkwardly in the entry hall, while Harlyn and I grab bags and weapons that Harlyn has already placed on the table. I sling a bag over my shoulder and pick up a couple of throwing knives, attaching them onto my belt. I have been studying them in Self-Defense. Surprisingly, I'm not too terrible.

"I see. Chase, darling, would you like to come choose a weapon?" Harlyn asks, strapping a wicked looking sword to her belt.

"Oh, sure." He comes into the kitchen and grabs a sword, strapping it to his hip. Harlyn claps her hands once.

"We are prepared as we can be, it's time to get going."

I hate that she's treating this like some picnic. Maybe it's her way of dealing. Maybe I shouldn't have asked her to come. She already has some sort of heart problem, and now I'm asking her to come on this mission? But I don't think I can do this without her.

We step outside and the cool air bites at my face.

"Chase, I need you to read my mind, then transfer the image I show you to Harlyn so she can take us there," I still have not fully begun to trust myself with the B.T. system, even though Blaze has been giving me lessons every day after school.

"Do you mind?" Chase asks as he goes to put his fingers on my temples.

I shake my head and his fingers press against my temples gently. I pull the image of the tiger statue and try to add as much detail as possible. Chase pulls his fingers away then places them on Harlyn's when she gives him consent.

She nods her head once she receives the image Chase got from my mind. I guess bringing Chase was the right decision. Harlyn takes our hands and we step into what I've been thinking of as the *danger zone.*

~

The first thing I notice is the smell. A smell of waste and rejected, rotting things. I cover my mouth with my hand, trying not to gag.

Right in front of us is the statue of the tiger, which is the same as the one in the picture. But now there is garbage lying in the streets around it. Neglected shacks line the pathways .

I had forgotten how much poverty the real world has. I glance at the other two. Chase is pale, and his fists are clenched. Harlyn has tears streaming down her face. She stumbles over to a mother and a child who are sitting in the dirt.

I run after Harlyn and grab her shoulders. "Harlyn, stop, it's okay. You can't help them."

"I-I didn't know," she sobs.

I should've thought about this beforehand. Bringing someone who has never seen hurt to this level then shoving them into the real world. She sucks in a breath and kneels before them. She waves her hands and light and water mix together to make golden water birds. They fly and float around the mother and daughter, who are gazing at her with wonder. She probably shouldn't do that out here in the open, but their happy faces make it hard to tell her to stop.

"It's time to go," I whisper to her.

She nods and unclips a golden necklace, which is sparkling with diamonds. She hands it over, then stands up. I take her hand in mine and pull out the compass with my other hand. It points north, in the direction of where the tiger's extended paw is pointing.

I wave for Chase to follow us, but he is still staring into space, a pained expression on his face. I sigh and go to him, taking his hand. I drag them along in the direction of the pointed paw.

The streets are cluttered with waste and hardship. I try not to look and tell the others not to either, but the hurt still slips into my vision. We have a mission. *I* have a mission. And my entire country depends on me succeeding.

We continue on along a dirt road for what feels like hours before we hit a jungle thick with green vines and exotic flowers. It rises like a green wall before us.

How can something this beautiful be so close to something so *not*?

I pull out my compass and it is still pointing north, straight into the thick green. I sigh and turn to Chase and Harlyn. "Okay you two, I need you to snap out of it. I know that was hard, and you might not be used to it, but we have to go. I'd like to get out of here before the sun sets.When we get back we can brainstorm some ideas for helping those poor people out." I point to the sinking sun.

Chase shakes his head and runs a hand down his weary face. "You're right. Come on Harlyn." He takes her hand and squeezes it. "Just think of something else." Her eyes focus on his face and she nods. He nods as well and turns back to me.

"Huh," escapes my lips before I can stop it. I've never seen this side of Chase before.

He raises an eyebrow at me. "Something wrong, Waterbug?"

I shake my head."Let's go. Harlyn, do you mind clearing the path? I'll come right behind you. Chase, you stay in the back. And keep your sword out."

They nod, and we fall into line. Harlyn waves her hands and light knives come out of her hands and slice a clean path. I prod Harlyn on, and we step into the dark forest.

The light grows dimmer and dimmer the deeper we get into the forest, and I get more and more terrified. The shadows look like monsters, ready to jump out and eat me at any second. Harlyn's flashing knives keep a steady *swish, swish, swish* echoing through the empty woods. The sound bounces off the trees.

Harlyn's face remains calm. Her posture is relaxed, in a way that suggests that she is ready for anything, but also ready to face it. I didn't know my adoptive mother was so fearless.

I clutch a knife in one hand and the compass in the other. I still check it even though the direction hasn't changed. I fall back and walk side-by-side with Chase.

"Do you find it strange that she didn't know people were hurting?"

Chase glances at me, a shadow in his eyes. "Yeah, the wealth they have, it could fix so much, fix our broken economy. Fix our world."

"I agree, maybe someday I'll talk with the Leaders about it. But I—"

He puts a finger to my lips. "Do you hear that?" Chase whispers. His hand drops away, and the jungle becomes silent.

"I don't hear anything besides water."

"I think we should walk faster," he says, and tightens his grip on his sword, knuckles turning white against the dark leather. He closes his eyes. And I realize he might be hearing thoughts.

I give Harlyn a frightened look, and she returns it. The knives slice faster, and I break into a sprint, close on Harlyn's heels. The sound of crashing water becomes louder. Suddenly Harlyn skids to a stop.

We stand right on the edge of a cliff, rocks from our feet crashing into the abyss below. I stop myself right before I crash into her. Peeking over her shoulder my breath leaves my chest.

Two hundred feet below is a raging river. To the right is a looming waterfall. At the top are two stone tigers, standing guard over something, front right paws pointing down. I check my compass and gasp at the change.

Words have formed on the metal top:

Follow the paws to where the water falls.

Of course, we have to go down the waterfall of doom.

"We have to go down there," I yell over the thundering water. Chase pales but nods. Harlyn does the same but squares her shoulders.

"Stand back! I've got this," she shouts. She closes her eyes and shoots her arms out. Water comes to her calling, forming a slide to the bottom. A small gap separates the slide from us.

"I'll protect you from the water at the bottom. Being hit by that much force would turn you into a pancake."

Of course, she has to add that. Chase nods and jumps, causing me to make a weird squealing noise. He shoots to the bottom and disappears in the spray.

You've got this, El. I hear Chase's voice in my head.

I run and jump, squealing for a second before hitting the slide. It shoots me down so quickly my breath leaves my chest.

The slide is odd, consisting of something that is solid and not at the same time. Like I'm sliding in sludge. I don't have time to wrap my head around how I'm staying on top of the water. The speed, water, and fear swallow up all thoughts. I scream, and I get water in my mouth.

Then it's all over, I've made it to the end of the slide. But that doesn't end my trials. I shoot right into Chase and send us sprawling across a stone floor.

"Graceful as always," Chase gasps as he helps me to my feet.

Though I don't know if my shaking legs can bear my weight. I choke and cough up water. He pats my back.

"You should've moved," I retort, choking again on the water that I inhaled.

"Yes, we should."

He pulls me to the side just in time. Harlyn shoots in and makes a graceful landing. I'm about to celebrate that we all made it this far alive, when she turns to me, horror in her eyes.

"They're coming!"

CHAPTER 22

STONES AND SHADOWS

"Who?" I ask, her alarm is contagious.

"Them. The Shadow Flectes." Suddenly I can't breathe. I clutch Chase's arm, needing something to keep me grounded.

"Oh, no. Them?" Chase asks. I suck in a breath. It's time for me to be strong.

"You two guard the entryway. I'm going to get the stones."

Harlyn nods once and they pull out their swords, standing ready at the entrance.

"Please be safe," I whisper and spin on my heel racing through the tunnels. There are smaller caverns on either side of me, and I check each one of them as quickly as I can. I sprint for about five minutes and silently thank my Self-Defense instructor for pushing me into shape, although rushing adrenaline is also helpful.

I skid to a stop when I finally spot a glowing yellow jewel the size of an egg. It stands on a pedestal in the center of the room. I rush in and grab it, slipping it into one of my pockets. I sprint out and find another jewel, which is a light teal color, in the next chamber.

This place is unguarded, it's too easy. I collect the fifth and final stone and skid out of the room, hope filling my heart. The green stone pulses brightly as I slip it into my pocket with the other stones.

But something troubles me. There seems to be no defense system here besides the waterfall.

I'm about to start heading back, when I hear a deep guttural growl from behind me. The sound is like explosive thunder smashing in the clouds. I whip around and spot three pairs of glowing yellow eyes like spotlights in the dark, pinning me down. I pull three knives from my belt and back up slowly. Desperately, I try to remind myself that running will only make my situation worse.

I squeeze my knives as three stone tigers step out of the shadows. Stone tigers at least twice the size of the average tiger, which are not small themselves.

Their golden eyes seem to be saying "lunch." I slide my knives back into my belt slowly, deciding they won't be very helpful under the circumstances. I'm going to have to attack with light. I slam my wrists together and twist them, reenacting what my Irradiation Bending teacher did to form a forcefield.

My heart leaps when light comes alive and surrounds me. Pundit Cora, though trying to fail me, has taught me well. My chances of survival are higher with this shield. I wonder if there's a way to shut them off.

I don't have time to think about it. The three tigers attack at once. They lunge at my forcefield and tear at it with iron claws. I grin at them and lift my hands, forming an X with my arms.

I slice down, and two beams of light come out and slice through the forcefield at two of the tigers. The light tears through the stone. They crumble to the ground, dust rising in the air.

My forcefield sputters, and crumbles. I am left unprotected. Right as the tiger is about to lunge, I dive out of the way. The tiger flies over my head. I pick myself up and twist my fingers together in the way my teacher had taught me.

The tiger stalks closer, yellow eyes staring intently into mine.

A lasso of light erupts from my fingers and curls itself into my hands. The tiger lunges as I swing my lasso. I fling it around its neck right as it pounces. I feel claws scrape down my back as I pull the lasso tight, slicing off its head.

I crumple with it. The pain in my back is crippling. It slices through my very being. Blackness creeping in at the corners of my vision. My black tunic is in shreds.

The feeling of my blood running down my back, hot and sticky, makes me sick. Picking myself up, I stumble along the passage as fast as I can. Chase and Harlyn need me.

I leave a trail of red behind me as I stagger along. Death feels close at hand. My blood leaves a red trail behind me. I am going to die. The amount of times I have said that in my fifteen years is slightly depressing.

I push myself into a painful sprint and hear the sounds of metal on metal echoing from up ahead. And battle cries. They are terrifying sounds. Bursting into the entry cavern, I find Chase and Harlyn battling three darkly cloaked figures. Two lie crumpled on the ground, red sits in puddles around them.

Their blades clash together. Light and shadows clash together.

Shadows erupt from the fingers of the people in the dark cloaks. One is about to slice Harlyn in half when I rush in and block it with a forcefield of light. It's becoming my favorite new defense mechanism. I catch a glimpse of startled sky-blue eyes.

Guilt and terror rush through me when I realise I left Chase out there with three Shadow Flectes. They turn on him like wild beasts cornering their prey.

"Stay here," I order Harlyn and jump out.

Sprinting towards Chase, I release a wave of raging water at them. It knocks Chase down, but it also takes out the Shadow Flectes. The water sends them sprawling.

I rush towards Chase, kneeling beside him. His eyes are closed. Terror flashes through me.

"Chase!" I yell, shaking his shoulder. I hold him up, and pull the water from his lungs. "Chase, please wake up." Tears come to my eyes. A deep slash across Chase's eyebrow leaves blood running down his neck. I attempt to wipe it away.

The Shadow Flectes are picking themselves up. Readying themselves to fight again.

Chase coughs, his sea blue eyes opening.

I smile, holding him close. "Thank the light, I thought you were dead."

"I'm not," he chokes, picking himself up. "But we really gotta kick these guys back to their island before that actually happens."

"I agree," I say, standing. My back screams in protest. I won't give up now.

We stand back to back. I pull knives out and fling them at the Shadow Flectes, quick as light. At that moment, I thank Pundit Clay for drilling me again and again.

My knife hits one in the stomach and they fall over. Chase's sword flashes so quickly I hardly have time to register where it's going until it collides with something in a soft thunk. I try not to gag as blood splatters our clothes. The red stickiness shocks me.

The last Shadow Flecte is beating back Harlyn's attempts at fighting. The force field has fallen. Her defenses are down. The last Shadow Flecte throws a knife and it catches her in the leg. She buckles with a cry of pain.

"We have to go!" I scream at Chase as he rushes the last Shadow Flecte, sword raised. But the last Shadow Flecte disappears into the shadows before Chase reaches him.

Chase nods. "You're going to have to get us out of here, El."

He scoops up Harlyn with surprising strength and slings her over his shoulder quickly but gently. I grab his hand and concentrate on keeping us together and think of home, which is the only place I can think of in my weakened state. I try not to listen to the groans of the dying Shadow Flectes around me as I press the center of my ring.

CHAPTER 23

HANG IN THERE, MURIEL

We fall into my yard from at least ten feet in the air. Pain ricochets up my legs and spine. I hear groans from the other two.

I really have to work on my landings. But at least we made it.

We're alive. But only by a little.

I try to stand but I've lost too much blood. Breathing becomes hard. Blackness crowds my vision. Stars dance in front of my eyes.

"Blaze, get Blaze," I groan. The pain in my back seems to be pulling me down. It feels numb, which makes me fear if I will ever be able to walk again. Footsteps retreat then come pounding back.

"Carry El, I'll get Harlyn."

Strong arms scoop me up and cradle me against their chest. The smell of home and fresh rain fills my senses. I catch a glimpse of ocean blue eyes filled with terror.

"Hang in there, Muriel. Please." Then the blackness takes over my vision and the world slips away.

~

"She's waking up!" someone shouts.

Voices are hushed. I blink my eyes open against the bright lights. The first thing I notice is a dull ache in my back area. I feel for my ribcage and find soft bandages.

Groaning, I attempt to sit up. Black spots crowd my vision. My head spins. The world tips. I let out a shuddering breath and feel hands slide into my own.

"It's going to be okay, Muriel, just sleep." Someone presses a vial to my lips, and I slip away once more.

~

My dreams are haunted by golden eyes and black cloaks. Screams echo off cavernous walls that I am unable to find the end of. I am trapped. The walls begin to leak blood.

"Call on the water from within you," a sweet voice sings.

The words bounce off the walls. I try to call on the water but can't. It fills me up, closing off my vision. The water swallows me up, and I am left in suffocating darkness.

~

This time, in the light, I fully regain consciousness. I open my eyes and focus on a small globe of light floating above me. I lift my head to find four people asleep in chairs in front of my cot. Chase and Ri hold my hands, their heads resting on my cot in a peaceful slumber. Ty and Devlyn are curled up in chairs. The fact that they're here, now makes me feel closer to them than ever before.

I glance around. Two cots away from me, Harlyn rests, her leg in a bandage up to her hip. Blaze sits beside her, also sleeping.

Of course, I woke up in the middle of the night. That's when I notice it. My bandages are gone. The pain is gone, as well. Whoever the doctor or physician was, I need to thank them.

"Hey, Waterbug," Chase whispers, making me jump. Surprisingly, Ri doesn't wake up. But she is one of the heaviest sleepers I've ever met.

"Oh, hi. How did you…." I notice he doesn't let go of my hand. Heat spreads to my cheeks.

"Know you were awake? I was monitoring your thoughts to watch if you were waking up. And here you are. In the middle of the night." He winks, and I smile back. He's one of those people that once you get to know them, you'd want to be their best friend.

"How are you feeling?"

"Too good to be true." I arch my back. No pain. I notice stitches in his eyebrow. "Your eyebrow."

"Oh yeah, it's nothing. It'll just leave a pretty sick scar once it's gone."

I grin. "Yeah it will. What happened to Harlyn?"

"Oh, the knife that got thrown at her had this poison on it that breaks all of your bones around it. Her femur."

I cringe. Now *that* is pain. "Oh, ouch." The understatement of the century.

"They've kept her under for the last week."

"Week? Are you serious?" All that time wasted. "The stones? School?"

"Yes, I'm serious. The Leaders got the stones. And you have a lot of catch up work to do."

"You've been here every night?" I ask, guilt crowding my head. I feel bad that I took that much time from their lives.

"Yeah, it's not that bad. And we haven't been wasting our time. We just come here to sleep every night. We're your personal cheerleaders! Even when you're sleeping!"

"You can stop monitoring my thoughts now," I say.

"Oh right, sorry." He looks down. "I'm glad we're best friends."

I try not to groan. "Those were *my* thoughts, Chase! And those were thoughts of a drugged, delusioned, sleepy person."

Ri stirs at my outburst.

"But, you don't deny them," he smirks. I sigh. "Friends at least?"

"Fine, friends," I grumble.

"I'll work 'best' in there eventually." He smiles. "Now go to sleep, it is back to school for you tomorrow."

"We'll see." I smile.

But before I drift off I hear, "Thanks for saving my life, Waterbug."

CHAPTER 24

RAGE, RED, WISH I WAS DEAD

"Um…Muriel?"

I jerk out of sleep, eyes wide. Ready for attack. None comes. Instead I notice a red-headed girl, sitting nervously at the foot of my bed, her hands nervously twitching.

"Oh… hey, Neva." I shift to sit up in bed. She cringes with each movement I make.

"I-I'm glad you're okay, and I came to give you this," she stutters and shoves an emerald green box at me.

"Oh," I say, slightly surprised. "Thanks." I open it and find five Lemon Bursts, slightly crumpled in on themselves.

"*Yes*," I say and sigh happily. "I've been craving these, well I always crave them. They're just so good! Ah, anyway, thank you."

Neva cracks a grin and her shoulders relax. "Um… was it scary?" She tucks her red curls behind her ears. "Being out there. With *them*?"

I nod slowly. "The Shadow Flectes are… intense. But I felt like the Shadow Flectes were kids, like Chase and my age, which is weird, right?"

Neva glances at me, brows pinched, then away again. She must find the floor pretty interesting, because she likes to look at it a lot.

"Yeah, that is strange.... But it could be the twins. The prince and princess Shadow Flectes." Neva shrugs.

I look at her with confusion and shake my head.

"We learned about them this week in Zilliad History, you just, um, missed it." She tugs at her curls.

"Oh, whoops. Almost dying does kind of make it hard to go to school."

Neva lets out a soft laugh at this. "I'm sure it does," she says, smiling. Her bright blue eyes sparkle, but there is something dangerous there. Something that could be triggered into an explosion.

"I'm just glad I took Chase instead of Ri," I say and exhale.

Neva's eyes harden, her posture rigid. "What do you mean?"

"Oh, it's just I had chosen Ri to go first with me, then I decided to take Chase." I shrug. "It kind of happened by accident."

"Oh," Neva scowls. "Ri has really been wanting to go on a mission."

I raise an eyebrow. "Oh, I didn't know that."

"I know you don't know that. But I think it's time you start taking other people's feelings into consideration." She hangs her head. "It's time for you to start caring for others, or you'll end up being a super selfish hero."

I slink back from her harsh words. I don't even understand where that came from. Blinking away tears, I pull the covers up to my chin. Hoping to hide myself.

I really have been a terrible friend recently. But I don't know what to do.

~

My friends wait for me outside the changing room, chattering. Blaze had brought my uniform and book bag by that morning, along with a heaping pile of homework.

Apparently where I have been staying is a larger branch of the hospital in the school. It's called the Ward.

I check my back for scars and there are only faint white lines.

I step out of the changing room and my friends grow silent. Ash rushes forward and hugs me tight. I flinch, ready for the sting of my back, yet no pain erupts.

"I'm so glad you're back," she says, her voice muffled by the fabric in my shoulder. She steps back and grins at me. "Sorry I couldn't join the nightly sleepover. My parents wouldn't let me." She tugs at the sleeves of her long-sleeved shirt.

"Me too," I say, squeezing her hand.

"How are you feeling?" Devlyn asks. Ri stands behind Chase, staring at the ground.

"Good. I just want to get to school and try to forget."

They nod. I decided earlier that I'm not going to tell Ri that she was originally the third person. It might cause a rift. But now she knows, and it obviously did. Why couldn't I have held my tongue with Neva?

Chase comes over and slings an arm around my shoulders, breaking me out of my thoughts. "Ready to be out of the hospital, Waterbug?"

I grin at him and nod. His ocean-blue eyes twinkle.

Ty drapes his arm around me, too, and I almost fall over from their weight. Devlyn chuckles and I grin.

"I'm glad you're back, Muriel Wiley," Ty says, his sky-blue eyes twinkling.

We exit the building and press our rings. I'm alive. We secured the stones. Harlyn is healing. Except Ri still hasn't said anything. Her cheeks are flushed with anger. She stares at the ground. And I don't know how to fix it.

~

In the courtyard, before we board the Levonos, people congratulate me on recovering the stones and on the fast recovery. Ty whispers to me that Chase had gone around bragging about my heroic deeds. I blush and turn away, wishing I could go back to when I was anonymous.

School is a mental reset, letting me know that things are really going to be okay. Irradiation Bending is as boring as always, though I try to pay extra attention to the special skills. After all, the skills saved my life.

The fact that Pundit Cora still glowers at me from over her desk, makes me strangely relieved. At least she isn't treating me with a celebrity status. During our experiment time, I make a small golden bird, slipping a bubble of water into the center like a small jewel.

I string it on a golden chain and slip it into my pocket. I'll find the right person to give it to eventually. At lunch, Ri and Neva don't sit with us. Instead, they sit with Rosie Halickle and some of her friends. I poke at my food, suddenly losing my appetite.

Tribe Training is taken to another level today. We are told that we are going to be fighting as a team, not just talking. For the past month, we have only been talking. Now it is time to start incorporating our Self-Defense skills into a team setting.

I am half-relieved and half-nauseous, battle-jitters filling my stomach. I have just recovered from a fight. But maybe that is what Pundit Lee is intending. If we are going to be the Protectors of this world, we had better have more training than the rest of the population. And be ready to bounce back and keep going after each battle?

"Pupils, choose your weapons." Pundit Lee, stands at the forefront of the room, hands folded in front of her. She presses a button and a rack of different weapons comes out of the wall. I grab a belt of throwing knives, trying not to remember how I had killed someone with this kind of weapon. Black cloaks, shadows, and red splatters on grey walls flash in my mind. I shake my head, it's time to focus.

Pundit Lee instructs us to stand in a line as she presses another button. Gears and metal grind against each other as something rises from below. I exchange nervous glances with my friends.

Two doors on the far side of the room swing open slowly. I hold my breath. Ten mannequin-like things stand in neat rows. They have red circles painted at different places about their bodies.

"Aim for the red circles. This lesson will commence now." The mannequins whir to life. Metal knives come out of their fingertips.

"Sweet, Wolverine robots." Chase pulls his sword out with a grin.

"What?" Devlyn asks, gripping his double-sided spear.

"It's a human thing. A superhero from a long time ago."

Devlyn looks lost, but he doesn't say anything else.

All of a sudden, the mannequins rush forward and I just have time to fling one knife when they're on us. I pull out a dagger and slash, aiming for red. I take down three before I realize that I am in action. I join Devlyn, who is fighting two surprisingly vicious machines.

I tell him I'll take one and fight it back. One slices at my chest, but I dive under its legs and stab it in the back. It sparks and falls over. Devlyn finishes his, as well. I spin around and find Ri battling one on her own. Ty and Chase have the last two.

I just decide to let them handle it when a scream echoes through the room. I've heard that kind of scream before. It echoes in my nightmares. And in a cavern under a waterfall. My stomach drops. I spin around and find Ri, kneeling on the ground, the mannequin's knives in her stomach.

Before I can even think, I sprint towards her, jump over her head, the warm rush that always comes during moments of adrenaline rushing through my veins. I cut off the mannequin's head. It falls away, wires sparking.

I turn back to Ri, who has a scary pool of blood spreading around her. Ty and Chase are still battling their mannequins. Devlyn stands beside me, shocked.

"Someone get a medic!" Devlyn yells, snapping out of his trance. Chase glances back at me, his eyes wide as he sees Ri.

"I'll get the medic!" He cuts off his mannequin's head then sprints away to get a medic. I kneel in the blood, holding Ri's hands.

"You're going to be okay," I whisper.

How could I have forgotten about her? Ri, who was always there for me. And now, when I should've been there for her, I wasn't. And I haven't even had the chance to apologize for… everything.

She stares at the ceiling, her face so pale, so void of color. Her hands are sticky from the blood. I hold back tears as her breaths rattle in her chest.

The hand of the mannequin is still inside of her, buried in her chest. The knives barely missed her heart. If I pull it out it will only make it worse.

Pundit Lee rushes in with Chase and two medics with a stretcher. They come over and scan the scene. The medics lay Ri on the stretcher gently and wheel her away.

"El, you need to get out of the blood." Someone grabs my hand and leads me away. I am sat down on a hard seat. My sobs come, echoing through my ribs. I almost lost Harlyn and now my best friend. I can feel her slipping through my fingertips, leaving me.

Someone wraps their arms around me and I cry into their neck. The tears dry up eventually, and I pull away from my comforter.

"It's going to be alright," Ty says, grabbing my hand. I hold on tight, wiping away the tears from my cheeks with my other hand. Chase and Devlyn stand, shocked into silence.

"No, it's not!" I clench my hands in anger, pulling away from Ty. "She almost *died*! And Pundit Lee let it happen! She left us there alone! *We're only kids*!"

Ty recoils at my outburst but doesn't disagree. And Harlyn. How many people are going to almost die…or actually leave us, because of the Leader and her plans for a bunch of kids to "protect" her magical perfect kingdom?

"You're right, El. That was very wrong of her." Ty sighs and places his head in his hands. "She just overestimated what we could do."

"I know." I try to take calming breaths. "But Ri…I mean some of us weren't up for the challenge."

"There isn't anything to justify what she did, but we should really go check on Ri." Ty stands up and extends his hand, pulling me up. We go to leave and Pundit Lee comes forward, looking apologetic. I can hardly look at her.

"I am so sorry I thought she could…." she stammers, her face deathly pale. Guilt filling her eyes.

"That was too high of a level for her. And now she's *dying*." My voice cracks multiple times. Pundit Lee is knocked back a step by my rage. I can feel it, too, rippling off me.

"I understand, I will leave you to it, then."

She backs away, slightly wilted. Did she really expect me to accept her apology? I try to leave, but Devlyn steps in front of me. He grabs my arms, scowling. His grey eyes stormy.

"Muriel Wiley." His voice is deep and scolding. "How dare you talk to a Pundit in that way?"

I rip my arms out of his grasp and scowl right back at him. "How dare I? *How dare I?* She almost killed my best friend!" I feel tears rising again.

"She was following the curriculum set by the Leader herself, for the Protectors! It wasn't her fault!"

"Don't speak her name to me right now, I just need to make sure Ri is okay."

He stares at me, rage in his eyes. "Think about this, we wouldn't want one of the *precious* Protectors expelled."

I scoff. "We wouldn't want them murdered either, or is my friend expendable?"

Devlyn's eyes flash dangerously. "Remember your place, *Muriel Wiley*." He turns on his heels and stomps away.

Chase and Ty glance at me nervously, not saying anything. I glance down. My uniform is covered in blood. My hands are a rusty red shade. What am I becoming?

"Let's go see Ri," I say.

Chase, Ty, and I race out and speed through the halls. We follow Chase, who seems to know the way. He's probably following the thoughts of the people who had just been in the room. *Telepaths.*

We twist through the halls and finally hit a door that has the words "Ward" above it. Chase pushes through the door, and we come into the waiting room. I try to push through the door that leads to the procedure room, but Chase grabs my shoulders.

"Not now. Sit down."

He holds a responsible, sensible air in his voice, so I decide not to argue. I shake off his hands and fall into a chair, twisting my fingers.

Of course, she had to get hurt. Right when everything was getting better. More tears begin to fall. Tears of someone who has given up.

Suddenly the door bursts open, Pundit Alora rushes in, looking worried. She hurries over to me and grabs my hands, kneeling before me. Her dark skin has a pale sheen to it.

"Are you all right?" she asks, brushing a tear off my cheek. It's such a motherly touch, that my heart clenches in pain. If only Harlyn were here, and not in the hospital with a shattered bone.

"I'm all right," I mutter, and hang my head.

"Come with me, Muriel Wiley."

CHAPTER 25

A SHADOWY PAST

My mind is so numb that I don't even think twice when I say, "Sure." I stand and follow her out the door, casting a look at the boys. Their faces show confusion, but they don't say anything.

Pundit Alora leads me along passageways, through corridors, at last stopping at a wooden door, with a wave encrusted in it. She pushes through, and the sound of running water hits my ears.

A desk covered in scrolls sits at the back of the study. The walls are covered in books. But above us water plays through the air. Water has always been a joyful thing for me. But now it actually *looks* joyful. It twists and twirls. Chasing the drops in silver twists and coils. It's alive.

"Wow, how do you manage to keep it up there?" I breathe as I settle into one of the plush armchairs in front of her desk. The wonder of it takes my mind off my problems.

She settles into her chair and sighs, "A lot of practice. You will learn one day that you can split your mind into many different places. The brain is the most powerful entity in this world, is it not?"

"Yes…."

"So once you learn to embrace that, you will learn to do things that are out of this world. We are masterpieces, created to create beauty and hope to serve the True Light. I hope to teach you that." Her grey eyes sparkle with knowledge.

"Huh," is all I say. My aquakinetic teacher is so intelligent and powerful. Things that I wish I was, but will probably never come to be.

"The reason I brought you here, Muriel Wiley, is that I have something for you. Something that will help you in the future, for your future is not going to be an easy road." She pulls from a pocket in her cloak a small wooden box, two knives crossing each other engraved into the top. She moves some of the scrolls and sets it before me. I glance up at her and she raises her eyebrows, challenging me to open it.

I slide my hands along the smooth surface. They bump over the swords. I click the latch open. Pushing the lid up, I find a silver necklace, two knives crossing each other with a charm in the shape of a circle.

"It was your mother's," Pundit Alora whispers, a smile pulling at her cheeks.

My mother. The words are like drops in a peaceful pool. Hope ripples through me.

I run my fingers along the delicate chain. "It's beautiful, thank you."

"It is not just beautiful my dear, it is a weapon. Put it on," she orders gently, watching me intently.

I pull the necklace out of the velvet case and unclasp it, then re-clasp it around my neck, moving my long hair out of the way. I notice that the Crownpass is gone.

"Tap the circle with the knives twice," she whispers, anticipation on her face.

I slowly raise my hand and tap the cold silver twice with my pointer finger. Black begins to grow out of it and my eyes widen in fear, my brain firing off a thousand reasons why I should yank off the necklace.

But I don't. I just watch. And wait. The black mist encircles me and then disappears, leaving a black and silver vest. It feels powerful on my skin.

"Ask for a knife." Pundit Alora is sitting calmly, her hands clasped on the table.

"Knife, please?" A knife pops into my hand, sleek, silver, and shining. "Whoa."

"Your mother had good taste. She wore that into battles. Fought for her land with that. And she told me she would like for you to have it."

"You knew my parents?" I ask, hope blooming in my chest. Curiosity is mixed in, as well.

"Yes, I did, child. I was one of your mother's best friends."

Someone who had known my parents. Someone who had talked with them, laughed with them, fought with them.

I smile at her, running the knife blade through my hands. I put it back into the vest, just by touching it to its surface.

"Now, how to deactivate it, you just tap the necklace once."

The necklace is melded with the vest, but the charm still remains at the neckline. I do as she says, and it disappears in a swirl of black smoke. It left, just how it had come. "Perfect, now, it is time for you to get back to your friends, for they will be worried about you."

I stand up and bow my head. "Thank you. Is there any chance we could talk some more?"

"Yes, when the time is right, you will learn more. Now go, child, your friends need you. This world needs you."

CHAPTER 26

WATCH YOUR BACK, EL

When I get back to the Ward everyone is gone except for Devlyn.

"They told us to go home, and I decided to wait and tell you."

I have a hard time looking at him after our fight.

"Thanks." I finger my necklace. Devlyn's eyes dart to it then back to my face. He gives me a small smile, almost apologetic.

"What'd Pundit Alora want?" He asks.

"Why do you ask?"

"She wouldn't ask to talk to you if there wasn't something important." Devlyn says, stepping closer. "Something that would help her get something."

I raise an eyebrow. "She's not like that."

"What if we're just friends?"

Devlyn laughs. "What I'm trying to say is, she is not just friends with people." He pauses, eyeing me. "Just watch your back, El."

"Okay…." Pundit Alora has always seemed kind and wise to me. She has never seemed mean or scheming.

Devlyn's warnings don't sink in. "I should be getting home. Any news on Ri?"

Devlyn shakes his head."No, but I'm sure she'll be okay. Good bye, Muriel." He steps away, and bows his head, disappearing into the hallway.

~

When I get home, it feels strangely empty. The gap where Harlyn should be is large and gaping, like the pain in my chest. Blaze is gone as well, making the house completely silent.

I slump into my living room and flop onto the couch, feeling the need to cry. But the gaping hole in my chest makes me feel empty, hollowed out. Like a shell.

Staring at my Conveyer, I wait for a message, telling me that Ri is going to be fine. No news comes.

I start on my homework, practice throwing knives with my new necklace. It feels so natural using it.

Suddenly my Conveyer buzzes, I whip it out and read the message: Ri is awake. She would like to see you.

Not changing out of my sweaty clothes I call for the Ward and let myself dissolve.

~

Racing through the halls of the Ward, I look for the number *59* over a door. Ri had been moved to the bigger Ward so that she could get more advanced care. It scares me how close to death she was.

I come to number *59* and screech to a stop, almost falling over. Righting myself, I straighten out my crumpled tunic and pull my hair into a messy bun. I grab the golden bird necklace from my pocket, now knowing what to use it for.

I knock and the faint voice of Ri drifts through the door, "Come in."

I take a deep breath, preparing the apology speech I layed out for myself in my mind.

Telling myself not to cry, I turn the door handle, and step quietly into the room, eyes on the floor. I can't seem to bring myself to look at her. It will be like looking in the face of all of my mistakes.

"El?" Ri asks, her voice shaking.

I nod, glancing at her for just a moment. A moment too long. Her entire torso is covered in white bandages, face deathly pale. Her hair is tied back from her face, which looks strangely hollow.

"Ri..." I say, not quite knowing how to begin. So instead I rush forwards and take her hand, trying to be as gentle as possible. "I'm so so sorry, if I had known that those robots would be so deadly I would have said something. And if I had known that you wanted to come on a mission I would have let you! You mean more to me than anyone else here. It's killing me knowing that you are in pain. And basically, I'm just very sorry. Everything's been so weird ever since we got here. And I miss my best friend."

"I miss you too, El." Her large grey eyes well up with tears. "And I understand, it's just hard for me to see you hanging out with other people. I'm just not used to it."

I laugh quietly. "I didn't really have friends before, did I?"

Ri shakes her head. "It just means that you belong here, El. And it's been so so hard for me. Adjusting to all of this. I don't think I belong here."

"Of course you belong here, this is who you are. Who we are."

"See, El, that's the problem. I don't belong here and I never will. Neva is the only one who gets it because she feels the same way. You're off with your little Flecte friends while I'm just trying to cope with all of this." Her eyes have turned hard.

"Ri...help me understand. I want to understand."

"No," she whispers.

Her words cut into me. "What do you mean, 'no'?"

"I mean, no. I don't think this is going to work anymore. Or ever again.We're just too different."

"Please, don't do this."

Ri shakes her head, resolved. "This is how it has to be. You are too dangerous to be around. Good bye, Muriel."

I shake my head. "No, I won't give up on you like this. I understand, I'm a terrible friend but we've always been against the world, together."

"I don't want to get hurt any more. Please Muriel, this isn't easy for me either."

Tears leak onto my cheeks. "Fine. But I won't give up on you." I pull the bird necklace from my pocket. "I made this for you," I whisper, holding it out.

She takes it from me, reluctantly. "Thank you. Now please go, this is for the best."

I nod, barely even registering what was going on. I back away. "Ri, I'll always be here for you. Whenever you're ready again."

Running out of the room and down the halls, I search for Harlyn's room number. Finding it, I slam into the room and collapse next to her bed, my head resting on the chair next to the bed. I take Harlyn's cold hand and hold it. My body is shaking with sobs.

My best friend left me. She basically told me that she hates me. And I don't know how to fix it.

"Please wake up, I could really use a mom right now." I wait for her eyes to pop open, for her to brush away my tears and hold me close. Telling me that it would be okay. But she remains silent, her eyes closed. Her breathing is steady but there is no color in her cheeks.

Another sob erupts from my chest. "I can't do this alone. I'm pushing everyone away and those closest to me are almost dying. How much more of this can I take?"

I wait again for her to wake up and give me all the answers. She doesn't move. I look at her leg, which is in a cast from her hip to her foot. It's propped up in a sling that is attached to the ceiling.

I squeeze her hand tighter. "I'm so sorry," I whisper.

I stay like that for a while, eventually drifting off into a nightmarish sleep.

A buzzing from my back pocket wakes me. I pull my Conveyer out, reading the message out loud, "The Leader is calling a mandatory meeting for all Protectors."

I almost throw the thing across the room. But instead I slip it back into my pocket and take a deep breath.

"Good bye, Harlyn. Things have to get worse before they get better." I pause and turn around before I leave the room. "At least I hope they do."

CHAPTER 27

CROWNS, LIES, AND SECRETS ON THE RISE

I followed the mandatory meeting message, to my chagrin. Being a Protector is supposed to help people. And all I feel like I've done so far is hurt them.

The castle that used to feel beautiful, now feels like walking into hell. Being here brings back memories from when it all began. Before my world was flipped upside down. There's a gaping hole where Ri should be. Her words still ring in my ears.

"Do you know what's going on?" I ask Devlyn as we begin across the trail. The fact that it becomes clear beneath my feet scares me less than when it happened to me the first time.

"I really don't," Devlyn says from behind me. "My mother has said nothing to me. But I'm sure it's extremely important, or else we wouldn't be here."

"Yeah... I hope everything is okay."

Ahead of me Ty mutters, "When is anything ever okay anymore?"

I can't help but agree whole-heartedly.

We come to the gate, where Lady Dez stands, her hands clasped firmly before her.

"Welcome children, come with me."

She leads us through the wide gates. My hands are shaking. What could be so wrong that I would have to come back here? Inside the throne room Leader Honora sits on her throne, golden and brilliant. And very intimidating.

I bow, my head lowered. "Lady Honora." My friends join me.

"Rise children."

When I look up, I notice Pundit Alora is standing next to Honora, hands clasped behind her back. I realize the striking resemblance between them.

"Children," Honora greets us again. "Thank you for coming on such short notice." Honora rises from her throne and paces forward to stand in front of us. I notice the boys tense beside me.

"There are two things we have called you here for." She meets my eyes, the deep grey holding a strange coldness.

"My sister will take you to place number one, and I will explain to you what is going to happen next."

I bow my head, showing I understand what Honora is saying.

"Sister, will you explain where you are to take them?" Honora re-settles herself on her throne, and Alora steps forward, her dark-blue dress swishing around her.

"After much talk with the Leader, we have decided to show you where you came from. Where you were born. We are not to tell you who your parents are…yet. That is for you to discover for yourself."

"Wait a sec," Chase says, holding up his hands. "My mom gave birth to me. I have a twin."

"That is what you were told, Chase." Pundit Alora takes his hands. "Everything happens for a reason."

Chase pulls away and glowers at her, his dark expression changing his looks completely. His eyes are haunted.

I hate the mysteries. I hate the lies. I don't trust *her*, the Leader who has been tugging me around on strings like a puppet. She is the reason Harlyn is asleep and won't wake up. She tore Ri away from me.

"Was that how it was for me, as well?" Devlyn asks, his dark skin tinted green.

"Yes, but you must keep this silent. The rest of your family mustn't know. You were born here, so we could keep an eye on you because we needed one of your Tribe to be from our valley, just in case the human experiments went wrong."

Lady Dez hangs her head. Devlyn looks like he's about to be sick. The same feeling fills my stomach.

"And the next problem? Just tell us and get it over with. I don't want any more drama later," Ty asks, changing the awkward subject. The word 'experiments' hangs in the air before me.

I want to know more about where I came from, but I have learned enough for today. Or at least for now. I was placed for Rolia to find. All of her stories had been a lie. She knew. It makes my stomach flip. The golden blanket she had 'found' me in was of Flecte material. No wonder I never saw it.

Honora steps forward again and stands next to her sister. "Shadow Flectes have been spotted on our shores. They are trying to get past our defenses. They want the stones."

Shadow Flectes. Invading our land. Trying to steal the foundation on which we are built.

"Not again," I groan.

"As our Protectors, we have decided to have you patrol the perimeter until they have decided to leave the idea behind. We must keep our stones safe."

"You want us to stay up all night and watch the perimeter?" I ask, laughing a little bit.

"Not all night. We will have two teams who will switch up. Ty and Muriel, Chase and Devlyn."

"So half the night," Chase confirms. Honora gives him an almost sympathetic look.

"Yes, but it is only for a couple of weeks. Until things calm down again," Pundit Alora says, smiling a little.

I sigh. Staying up half the night is going to be a lot. I already feel like I don't get enough sleep.

"What about Ri? She's a Protector as well," Ty says, and I nod. Her name makes my eyes burn. I won't cry here, I can't cry here.

Pundit Alora and Honora exchange a dark look that can't mean anything good.

"It is a great disappointment to us, but Ri is not strong enough to be a Protector. She will no longer be doing any missions with you," Honora informs us.

"But that's not fair!" I shout before I can think. "She hasn't even had a chance to prove herself! Just because that machine stabbed her doesn't mean she's not worthy! Yes, she doesn't want to risk her life. But this was the reason she had to be taken away from her previous life."

I feel a hand on my shoulder.

"Muriel, stop," Devlyn whispers. I'm about to shove him away before I remember who I'm talking to. I blow out, clenching my fists. This is not the time. Or place.

"Muriel, we understand your anger and disappointment. But Ri is not able to go on real missions if she cannot complete her Tribe Training without getting injured. You and Chase already completed a mission against the Shadow Flectes! And you survived. Riana will be able to complete school and will have a wonderful life. But without the responsibility." Honora steps away, probably sensing the smolder in my eyes.

"So she'll wake up to humiliation," I say. "You ripped her away from her family for nothing."

Honora nods slowly. "We did not intend for this to happen, but accidents do occur. We will be looking for a replacement for your Tribe."

They're protecting her. But also ridding her of the reason that she was born in the first place. I bow my head and take a deep breath, willing myself not to get angry. I feel tears rising in my throat. I swallow them down.

"All right," I say. "When do we start the perimeter guard?"

Distraction is my best solution to pain.

"Tonight. After Pundit Alora takes you to where you will be patrolling." Honora tugs on her sleeves.

"Ty and Muriel, you will have the first shift, starting at sundown. You will be relieved by Chase and Devlyn at midnight." We bow our heads. Accepting the instructions. "Bring your weapons."

We bow our heads again. This is what I was born to be. A Protector, guarding our world at all costs. Even if that means death, or betrayal to those I love.

Injustice boils just beneath the surface. I will hide it, until the time is right.

"Let us go see where you came from, I believe it is only fair," Pundit Alora says and takes our hands. She shouts, "Arenvale!" Honora fades away as Pundit Alora presses the center of her ring, whisking us away.

CHAPTER 28

THE ORIGIN

Humid air blasts my face as our bodies reform. I begin to sweat immediately. My dark hair clings to the back of my neck. My school uniform is way too hot for this weather. A squat stone building stands before us, abandoned and covered in vines.

"We were born there?" Chase asks, wrinkling his nose. "It's kinda… sad."

He's not wrong.

"Never judge a book by its cover," Pundit Alora tells him and walks towards the building. She moves some vines away from a panel that is inlaid in the stone and presses her hand against its smooth surface. A green light flashes around her hand, and a beep resounds through the empty jungle.

A hole opens up in the stone wall, widening until it is large enough to fit a human through. Pundit Alora goes first, leading the way. I follow her, my heart thumping quickly. This is where my life began.

Inside, it's cold and dark, a tiny bit stuffy, as well. I hear a click, and the room is filled with a soft yellow light. The walls are circular and white.

A glowing orb hangs from the ceiling like a giant egg. Then I spot them. Four tanks, with the form of a small human outlined in a green substance.

"Ew," Chase whines. "I was born in that green sludge?"

"Yes, Chase Cutler. Now stop whining."

I was thinking the same thing. The tanks are sad things. They are shaped like eggs and sit on white tables that have a bunch of weird buttons covering the surface around it. You would have to have high tech to grow a baby like a womb does.

"I think I'm going to be sick," Chase says, holding his stomach.

Pundit Alora steps back.

I walk forward to the third one in line and place my hand on the glass, studying the inside. Devlyn, Ty, and Chase start messing with the buttons two eggs down. They laugh when some of it bubbles to the surface. I can't understand how they are finding joy in this. Pundit Alora comes up beside me.

"This was yours." Her hand rests just next to mine. "I watched you grow into a child. Watched and thought of all the responsibility that was going to be heaped onto your shoulders someday. Watched and wished your mother could have been there as well." There it was, the hint at something that I can't quite grasp.

"My mother," I whisper. "What was she like? Why can't I know her name?"

“There will be many secrets uncovered in the future, child. But for now, it is best that you are left in mystery.” Pundit Alora places her hand over mine.

“She was beautiful, your mother. She looked a lot like you. Large green eyes, dark hair. Tall. And she was so kind and brave.” She closes her eyes in a silent memory.

I smile.

“She sounds amazing,” I say in wonder. A few tears fall onto my cheeks.“I wish I could have known her.”

“She was.” Pundit Alora takes my hand and squeezes it. “Every time I see you, I wish she were here as well.”

“Me too.” I glance down. “What’s happening to my adoptive mother, Harlyn? No one is telling me what is happening to her heart, I’m told we’re immortal. But it seems like she’s dying.” The words make my throat close up.

“‘She is suffering from a rare heart disease that targets only Flectes. It’s... very hard to cure and very hard on the body. The best thing you can do for her is pray for a miracle.”

I close my eyes and nod. “Thank you for telling me. Everyone has been so secretive. It’s hard to know who to trust.”

“Secrets are hurtful, but they can also bring harm if known. Have patience, child. Answers will come in due time.”

Pundit Alora takes her hand away and steps back as a rupture resounds from where the boys are. I glance over at them and put a hand to my mouth. They are covered in green slime. Pundit Alora rolls her eyes. I can’t help but laugh.

"It was Chase," Ty says pointing a green finger at the blonde boy in the middle, who smiles sheepishly.

"How was I supposed to know the button with a star on it was supposed to make it explode?" Chase asks.

"That star meant explosion," Devlyn says grumpily, wiping green slime from his eyes.

"Oh, ha ha." Chase smiles nervously.

Pundit Alora cracks a smile.

"Devlyn, I know this place does not mean anything to you, but since the rest of your Tribe was born here, I thought it was wise to bring you along."

"Thank you, ma'am. They are my other family. So it's right to go where they go."

His words warm me up. Family. Second family. Well, for me, it would be my fourth family. I've had four families.

"Well, children, it is time to return home. You all must get ready to protect the islands. And you boys must de-greenify yourselves."

I chuckle, and Ty's cheeks turn pink through the slime. Pundit Alora clicks off the lights, and we step back into the jungle. I bid my birthplace goodbye as we grab hands and flash away.

CHAPTER 29

INVISIBLE HANDS, AN UNPROTECTED LAND

I tap my ring and shout out "Coastina," where Ty and I agreed to meet. I reform on a dock as the sun begins to slip behind the horizon, decorating the skies in orange and gold hues. Waves lap at the wooden planks below my black boots.

I fiddle with the sleeves of my green tunic. My mother's necklace rests over the neckline. I grab it, and rub the outline, reminiscing about the things that Pundit Alora had told me about my mother. I wonder about my father as well; what was he like? I wish I could see them laugh, that I could hug them goodnight and laugh over something silly with them.

Homesickness fills my stomach. It's hard to belong somewhere when you don't even know who you belong with.

A noise behind me snaps me out of my daydream. Ty stands, a bow in hand, quiver over his shoulder.

"So, how are we supposed to do this?" I ask, and walk towards him.

He shrugs nonchalantly. "I don't know. But we probably should just watch the perimeter on this side...?"

"Your guess is as good as mine, let's go."

We head out of town and stick to the coastline, walking back and forth across the same stretch.

I wish Ri was here with us. I haven't even had a chance to go see her. And have had no updates. I miss the world where everything was normal. I shake my head, clearing the fog of the past.

We pick our way through a calm forest, the trees' low sweeping branches reaching for us.

"So, Ty." He glances over at me and raises an eyebrow. "Tell me a little bit about yourself."

He laughs lightly, in the calm way he always does.

"Let's see, where to begin..." He trails off, so it clearly was not a question for me. "I lived in Tacoma, Washington, for almost my whole life. I was an only child the whole time. My parents adored me. I was moderately spoiled." He laughs, then continues. "I went to a private prestigious school because my parents wanted to have the best for me. Wanted *me* to be the best. I liked the school they sent me to. It was strict and everything you think of when 'private school' comes to mind.

"Uniforms, dormitories, everything. I was the top in my class, had friends. But then one day my dad decided to move our small family to Ractia, California, of all places."

He sighs, then continues, "I'll admit I wasn't happy with his decision. We were already comfortable with our lives. I liked my school, my friends. I was happy.

"Dad claimed it was for the best, but I couldn't agree. But then everything happened with Chase, and you, and Ri. It all made sense. It had been planned from the beginning. Why they chose your town, beats me. Probably because you and Ri were there."

His chin drops to his chest. "I never got to forgive my dad. I never gave him a hug. Never said I was sorry when he had been right. Even when I went back, I was too blinded by what was happening to *me* to realize that he was probably hurt."

He shakes his head. "Never take any moments for granted, El, things can happen in the blink of an eye."

I lay a hand on his arm. "Your dad loved you. I'm sure of it. And love forgives all things."

He glances at me and nods slowly, a skeptical look in his eyes.

"Well, now that I shared my story, it's your turn."

I punch him. "I thought I was going to get out of it."

"Nope, I don't get to be all sappy with my life story then miss out on the great Muriel Wiley's." He smiles. I begin. Telling him about Rolia being my adoptive mother and finding me in the rain, how I was abandoned to live on my own. How everyone found me weird and out of place.

"Well, you're here now and you have plenty of people to love you. Besides, bullies don't get to define who we are. We define who we are."

"Aren't you just a walking quote book," I say, grinning.

"It's bad to deny who you truly are."

~

Months pass with school dragging by, the 'weeks' that Leader Honora told us about are forgotten as we complete our duty every night. My body becomes used to little sleep.

I try to avoid my house as much as possible, since Harlyn hasn't recovered yet. Every time I go into the kitchen it just reminds me of her and the mistakes I made. Blaze spends most of his time at the Ward and when he comes home he keeps to himself. I dive into my schoolwork and the distraction it brings.

Leader Honora brought Ash into our Tribe, noticing how much we hang out. Ri ignores us, and I don't know how to fix it.

The weather warms, and exams draw closer. I'm passing all of my classes except Irradiation Bending. Pundit Cora seems ready to fail everyone in class. She has it out for us. Pundit Alora has been amping up the intensity of our lessons, leaving me exhausted come the time when Ty and I need to scout the coastline.

A whistle blows high and clear, "Run another lap, Wiley, get a taste for how your sparkly, twinkle-toes unicorn feels!" Pundit Clay yells loudly from the stand overlooking the race track. Pundit Clay is my Cradestant coach, which is unicorn racing. But since he is also my Self-Defense teacher, he makes me run. A lot.

I puff around the sandy track, my boots sinking with every step. Blissia looks at me with an aloof air. I come back around and Pundit Clay nods at me. "That is enough for today, Wiley. Be studying for your exam, front snap kicks are gonna be a part of it."

I nod at him and grab Miss Bliss.

"I'll see you tomorrow, Pundit Clay."

But what's been bothering me more than the long nights is Ri. She woke up but hasn't come near us. She's been ignoring us completely. And what's worse is that she's traded us for Neva. Ri is really good at ignoring people. I've seen her do it before. I just never thought it would be directed at me.

One day at lunch, I walk over to her table and sit down across from her. The other kids sitting there shoot me cold looks.

"Hey," I say, deciding that was a good word to start the conversation.

She doesn't even glance up though when she says, "Why are you here?"

"Ri, I'm your friend."

"Are you?" Her words cut through me like a knife. I had thought that maybe there was hope. Maybe I could bring her back. But her tone was final. I was not her friend anymore.

"I'm always here for you, I just want you to know that." I slip out of the chair, not looking at her, and walk back to my table. I slide in next to Ash, putting my head in my hands.

"Did she say anything?" Ash asks.

I shake my head.

"If she doesn't want to try, don't give it any thought," Chase says from across the table.

I nod again. "I just can't believe she wouldn't try. She's been my friend forever." I feel tears rising in my throat. It's sleep deprivation again. I've never had a hard time not crying. But ever since I'm not sleeping enough, the tears have just started to come more easily.

Ash pats my back. "I know this isn't easy for you, but if she's not trying, you shouldn't give it any thought."

I nod again and leave the table, making my way out of the crowded cafeteria. Ri's words ring through my ears.

Maybe I am a really selfish hero.

~

"Tonight's the last night," Ty says, and I fight the urge to whoop.

Leader Honora just gave us the note of clearance this morning. I couldn't be more ready for anything in my life.

"Finally. I've never been this sleep-deprived." We sit back-to-back on the beach, books in hand, weapons at our sides, sitting in the sand.

We might have become quite relaxed guards after not seeing the grass move for months

"Same, it was fun getting to know you though."

I smile. It has been. "Not to sound mushy or anything, but I gotta say you're the older brother I've always wanted."

Ty laughs at that, his calm joyful laugh. "And you're the little sister I've always wanted." He nudges me with his elbow, and I hit him back.

We shou-" Suddenly the water blasts fifty feet into the air.

"Oh, light," I yell and scramble to my feet, tapping my necklace twice. Ty scrambles beside me, knocking an arrow on his bow. The water settles back down and three dark figures crawl out of the water, like sea serpents.

"I thought they didn't have water powers," I say to Ty, grabbing a knife.

"They don't."

The figures in black realize we're there a second too late. The water behind them ruptures again. But it's not their doing. A giant wave crashes over them and I pull them into the air in a giant bubble. Suddenly one of them disappears, and another creates flames that lick away at the bubble I have them in. My water evaporates and two of them fall to the ground. I can't find the third one who disappeared. Ty lets his arrow fly and it hits one of the figures in the stomach making them fall to their knees. The other figure hurls a ball of fire at Ty. I dive at him and send us sprawling across the sand.

"Thanks," he says and jumps to his feet. Suddenly invisible hands wrap around my throat. I try to scream out and knee at my captor, but I can't find anything to come in contact with. I call the water towards me and encase my captor and I in the bubble filled with water. I breathe easily, but the other person won't be able to last long. We stay there until I feel the fingers slip away from my throat.

Releasing my hold on the water, I land face first in the sand and it pulls me back to my senses. I can't spot the unconscious Flecte. They seem to be able to hold their invisibility even during sleep.

Fatigue claws at my chest, holding a bubble for that long drained me. Ty is battling the fire Flecte, dodging and deflecting the fireballs being thrown. Roots erupt beneath the fire wielder and incase them in a root prison, every time the fire burns some roots away, thicker roots take their place. Two down and an invisible one to go. I close my eyes and feel through the water in the ground for a presence. And they're slipping away. They're gone. They must have woken up and run for it.

I connect eyes with Ty and shake my head, signaling that I'd lost the invisible person. Ty gathers his roots and throws the fire-wielder into the water by slapping them across the chest with a broken off root.

I form a wave to wash away the person who is lodged with an arrow, bending the currents to carry them far, far away. I feel no guilt as I rush after the faint presence I feel in the ground.

CHAPTER 30

THE HOPE STONE

Ty and I race through the forest. If we fail, we might be demoted from Protectors. The whole reason I got ripped from Rolia will be for nothing. Ri leaving me in her spite was for this. And now I have Harlyn and Blaze. Harlyn and Chase nearly died for me.

I can't let them down.

I glance back and find Ty sprinting after me, brows knitted in concentration. Sweat pours down his face. He seems to be tripping a lot, which isn't normal. He's better on his feet than I am. Turning my attention forward again, I leap over a toppled tree just before I would have tripped over it.

The presence I'm tracking is faint, but is growing stronger as we sprint after it. They don't seem to be very fast. The woods seem to stretch on endlessly before us.

The hooded figure could be anywhere.

My chest heaves from sprinting for so long. I struggle to keep up my speed. But I repeat the names of those who care about me and I push myself harder.

The trees end as suddenly as they had come. I screech into the clearing, Ty right behind me.

A domed golden building stands at the center of the lush green meadow. Golden flowers spring up from the ground, giving off a delicious scent. Facets shaped in stars cover the top of the dome. My eyes travel over the building and catch sight of a figure.

My eyes fasten on them and I find, standing at the door, a beautiful girl. White hair twisted in a braid, black clothes bringing out the angles in her face. A glowing green jewel is clutched in her hand. My heart leaps as I recognize it. The Hope Stone.

"A little late are you, Muriel?" she hisses, laughing.

"How do you know my name?" I breathe out, trying to catch my breath. Unsure of what my next move is, knowing I need to stall and get that stone back.

"You're famous where I come from," she says, grinning again. Her smile is terrifying. Too put together for someone who was almost suffocated.

"We've been waiting for you, as well. My brother and I are excited at this new threat. Something worth our time. And you have proven more difficult to get through than we expected."

"You won't get through us," I say, teeth gritted. She laughs and twirls the stone she's holding in her hands. Throwing it back and forth. I grab a knife and hurl it at her head. She dodges easily.

A growl builds in my throat. She shakes her head and laughs again.

I'm too exhausted to pull any tricks out of the bag. We lost.

"Oh, but I already have." She winks then disappears, stone still clutched in her hand. Ty and I stand still for a moment. My breaths come short.

"We lost it," I whisper, mostly to myself.

"What are we going to do?" Ty asks, his voice shaky. I put my head in my hands, trying to calm myself down.

"We could lose our positions as Protectors," I mutter with a shake of my head as I try to clear the cobwebs from my thoughts. Everything seems to be moving in slow motion.

"We have to tell them," Ty says, and I nod. But when I face him, I notice something is wrong. His skin is ashen, sweat trickles down his temples. His hands are pressed tight under his ribs.

"Ty...." I say. He shakes his head.

"She got me," he says and removes his hand from his stomach.

Blood streams from underneath his hands. I clap my hands to my mouth, trying not to vomit. I rush forward and support him, slipping my shoulder under his.

"I'll get you out of here. Hang in there." I press my ring and call for the Ward.

~

"Your friends really love to get hurt," Dr. Dolan comments as he closes the door to the waiting room behind him.

"Is he going to be alright?" I ask, twisting my fingers tightly together.

"He will be." Dr. Dolan grimaces. "You need to go see the Leader, Muriel."

"How…?" I ask, narrowing my eyes.

"Do not be alarmed. I read your mind because of the state you seem to be in. And determining from your friends...condition. Something didn't go very well."

"I'm not in a state." I stare at him. "I'm just trying to understand what to do next." He had no right to read my mind. Even in these circumstances. He must've broken one of the Flecte Rules.

"You look like you got chewed up by a dragon."

"Why is that not the first time I've been told that?"

Dr. Dolan almost laughs. "I believe you'll do the right thing, Muriel."

"I'll go see the Leader." I push myself out of the chair. "And thanks for helping my friends. It means a lot to me. "

Dr. Dolan smiles sadly. "Go to Hearthstone, everyone is congregating there to figure out an answer to our predicament."

"Wish me luck." I sigh and press my ring, bracing myself for whatever is to come.

CHAPTER 31

I'LL COME BACK, I PROMISE

Voices come from inside even before I open the door. I push open the door, bracing for the fight I know is coming. The conversation goes quiet for a moment, then gets elevated again. I run into the living room and the conversation dies.

"Ah, Muriel. Sit down please," Honora says and turns back to Lady Dez, who is shooting me evil looks, the rest of the Eminence standing around her.

This is a moment when I wish I had the ability to disappear. I slowly walk down the two steps into the living room and sit down on a plush armchair. Devlyn and Chase glance at me, their eyes wide. How had they found out so quickly?

Blaze stands by the fireplace. I can't seem to be able to meet his eyes. If only Harlyn were here. She would hug me and tell me it is going to be okay.

I sit in the chair next to the fireplace, fidgeting for a moment. No one seems to be paying me attention, except Chase, and he just looks like he wants to know what I did.

I decide to speak up.

"What's going on?" I ask, raising my voice.

All four Eminence sigh as one. Honora runs a hand down her face. Yep, I'm in trouble.

"Muriel, what you have done will spiral our world into chaos," Lady Dez explains. Honora exchanges glances with her. "The Hope Stone is very crucial for our existence, and the humans. Without it, humans would have already killed each other and we would no longer exist. Hope is stronger than fear. But in the hands of the Shadow Flectes, it cannot spread the hope that it has. I hope you understand how very important that green rock is to our society?"

I let out an exasperated huff. "Why did you have it sitting out then?" My tone is probably too sharp for being the one to destroy everything.

"We thought our Protectors would do their jobs," Lady Dez snaps. I flinch.

"Patience. She is just a child." Honora steps forward and lays a hand on my shoulder.

"Muriel, what you have done is not something that can be undone. The Hope Stone is gone and in the possession of the Shadow Flectes, and the Shadow King, though we have not heard from him in centuries, I fear this might help him rise to power once more."

The mention of his name sends fear through my heart like a knife.

"I met him, once." I say quietly. The noise in the room dies with my words.

"You *what*?" Lady Dez says.

"I met the Shadow King, he confronted me before I came back to Zilliad." The words spill out. How I wanted to say something but it slipped my mind.

Time stands still for a second.

"And now it's too late to have warned you he was coming for us," I finish lamely.

Another beat of silence follows.

"There is nothing to be done but to do the next right thing," Honora finally says. "We just hope that next time, may the light protect you if that should happen, that you would let us know. We also need to protect this world. And the Shadow King is the ruler of seeking to destroy anything good that is left in this world."

The Eminence nod.

"I'm sorry, if I had said something..." I twist my fingers. Honora just shakes her head.

"The future is all that matters now. I just wished you would have told us."

"Yeah, you've been carrying that all these months?" Chase asks, his ocean-blue eyes wide.

I nod slowly.

"I can't believe you didn't trust us with that," Blaze says quietly. "Harlyn and I want to help you, El. But that's hard to do if you keep everything from us."

I hang my head, shame weighing heavier than it ever has before.

"It is too late now to go back. But there is something you can do to make it right. The Hope Stone must be restored." Honora glances at Blaze, he hangs his head.

"You mean, you want me to go get it? *From* the Shadow Flectes?" I ask, fear squeezing my stomach. Chase balls his fists, twisting the pillow he's holding, back and forth.

"Yes. Devlyn and Chase have been chosen as well because they have proven themselves worthy of protecting this land. And if you fail, you will be demoted."

Honora totally just took a dig at me. And I deserve it. After all I have kept to myself. After losing the stone.

Honora continues, "Ash is too new to the group and Ty is injured, therefore, it lands on your three's shoulders."

I glance at Chase and Devlyn and raise an eyebrow. Devlyn smiles reassuringly and Chase gives a thumbs up. Yet, they both look more terrified than I have ever seen them.

"When do we leave?" I ask, reverting my eyes back to Honora. She grimaces, and I know bad news is coming.

"As soon as possible."

"As in, right now?" I ask, twisting my fingers.

"Yes. Your adoptive father has already packed for you." Honora gestures to a bag sitting at the foot of the spiraling staircase. "We will leave you now so you may say your goodbyes. Amon will meet you in Coastina to send you out."

Honora bows to me as well as the rest of the Eminence. I don't quite know who Amon is, but I don't really care. All that matters now is proving that I can be trusted again. Not just by the Leader and Eminence, but by my friends and adoptive parents too.

Chase and Devlyn stand following the others out. Right as they are about to leave, I hear the brush of a thought in my consciousness. *Everything's going to be all right, El. Just trust.*

Chase doesn't look back as he sends the transmission, but I know it's from him. My nerves settle a tiny bit. I turn back to Blaze. "I wish she was here," I whisper. "I'm so so sorry. And I know I don't deserve to be forgiven, and you can kick me out if you'd like. I know I deserve it." Tears stream down my cheeks. I stare at the floor.

Two arms circle me and pull me close. I cry into Blaze's chest. "I'm so sorry, Dad."

He pulls back and smiles, his eyes gleaming with tears of his own. "I forgive you, and I always will. Because that's what love does. Harlyn loves you too, and she'll be better soon. When you come back she'll be here. We'll be here. You'll always have a home with us, Muriel. As long as you want one."

"Thank you." I hiccup and nod. "Tell her I'm sorry."

He nods. "I will, and I'll make sure Bliss is taken care of while you're gone."

"I'll come back. I promise." I owe this to them, to everyone.

"Don't make promises you can't keep, El," Blaze whispers, pain etched in his voice.

"I will come back." I step back. "I have to come back."

"We love you," Blaze says, surprising me even more than this unexpected journey. All along they had, even when I didn't feel it. I smile and feel a tear slip down my cheek.

"I love you, too," I whisper then turn away, grabbing my bag. He stands in the golden doorway as I drift away.

CHAPTER 32

WHAT'S A SQUIDARK?

I arrive in Coastina, the ocean city on a wharf. Salty wind blows back my hair. Chase and Devlyn are already waiting for me in their dark outfits, just like mine. They look solemn, and it's strange. Chase never looks solemn.

I go over and stand next to Devlyn and he puts his arm around my shoulders, holding me up. I catch a look of pain on Chase's face, but it quickly passes, replaced with a smile. Amon clears his throat from where he is standing on the pier. I reluctantly turn my gaze towards him.

"Children, we know this is very hard for you, but you are saving our world. We owe you our gratitude," Amon says, his deep voice almost getting lost in the sound of the waves.

He steps up to me and gives me a compass that will lead me there and back only once, and a flask that will not run out of water. He also hands me the Crownpass necklace, I put both items into my pack and clip the necklace around my neck. We wait for instructions, but he does not say anything else.

"Should we go or just stand in awkward silence staring at each other?" Chase asks with a smile, trying and failing, to lighten the moment.

"You should go. Best of wishes, children." Amon says and bows.

We bow to him and turn around, heading to the end of the wharf. Once we reach the end, I pull out the compass and string it on my mother's necklace. It clinks against the Crownpass The compass is about the size of a quarter so it doesn't weigh down on my neck.

"I don't think I'm ready for this," I say. Our toes stick off the end of the dock. The sun is beginning to set on the horizon.

"El, you're one of the bravest people I know. You got this."

"Thanks, Dev, but seriously. What if my bubble doesn't hold up? You guys would drown."

"Mmm, pleasant. But you got this, Waterbug. We won't drown as long as we're in your hands."

I blush from the compliment and take a big breath, closing my eyes and feeling for the water. The power of the ocean crashes into me, and I smile in spite of myself.

"I can do this," I say, mostly to myself.

I take both of their hands and yank them towards the water, which is twenty feet below. Flecte docks are higher than humans. Chase lets out a tiny scream which causes me to laugh, which causes us to plunge into the water without a bubble.

The water is freezing. My body seizes up and I almost don't form the bubble. Someone squeezes my shoulder, and I come back to reality. I spread my hands, forming a bubble around us. As soon as I do, I dry us off.

I have lost my breath and lie on the bubble's soft interior, exhausted. Chase and Devlyn are shivering too much to complain that I didn't make the bubble in time.

"I did it," I say, sounding a little shocked.

Chase glares at me. "You should warn a guy before you pull me off a dock and into the frigid ocean."

The bubble is about the size of a bathtub, so it is a little too tight with three people.

"Yeah, sorry," I say and close my eyes, willing the currents to carry us east.

Time slips by. The ocean rushes past us. Coral reefs, blue waters. We float just below the surface, but the waves above still toss us from time to time.

I don't know why the water by the dock was so cold. But the water around us doesn't feel like that. We enter an eerie valley that is formed by underwater mountains. Shadows and mouths of caves make the hair on the back of my neck stand up.

"I don't like this," I mutter.

Suddenly a force knocks us from behind. I fall forward, hitting my chin on Devlyn's knee. Pain makes my eyes sting.

"It's a SEA MONSTER!" Chase screams from my right.

I whirl the bubble around to find a giant sea creature that looks like a giant squid and shark mixed together. It's about the size of a semi-truck and has teeth the size of me. I count ten huge tentacles swirling the water.

"We're dead," Devlyn says, covering his face with his hands.

"It was nice knowing you guys," Chase mumbles, before he puts his hands together and mumbles delusional prayers.

"Stay here, I'll be right back."

"Be safe," Devlyn says.

"I'll try."

I jump and burst through the bubble's thin layer, instantly resealing it. Willing it away into some shadows of a hollow in the rock wall, I spin towards the monster, tapping my necklace twice.

Fear mixes with my adrenaline, and the feeling of danger laps at my toes. The creature bares its teeth, as if wondering why it got such bad luck on his appetizer size.

It must not care or it just needs a snack to brighten up its day because it bares its teeth and sends a large grey tentacle in my direction. I dodge out of the way, urging the currents to maneuver me. I barely manage to avoid being crushed into the gray rocks that line the walls of the sea floor as it snaps its tentacle towards me.

I ask for a long dagger from my vest and float, waiting, as the squidark, that's what I decided to name it, slashes at me with its razored tentacles. I burst towards the rocky ledge and guide the currents to channel me along it, just keeping ahead of the tentacles.

The squidark lets loose a roar and lunges towards me. I swivel between it's twirling tentacles, noticing they are lined with tiny teeth-like daggers.

Swimming to the other rock face, I gather my senses about me. I raise my knife and jump, adding extra power from the water in me to my legs. I propel through the water raising both of my arms to strike. My target is lined up right where I want it.

I stab it in its single eye. It slashes out at me but I hold onto the knife, dragging the blade down its body. I try to ignore the dark blood swirling around me. I kick off its body and spiral away, getting out of its way as it shudders and falls toward the murky sea floor. Its great, grey body sinks into the dark depths below.

Breathing a sigh of relief and swimming to where I hid the bubble, I find the boys' faces pressed against the film trying to find me. Chase notices me coming over and points, "She's alive!"

I slide into the bubble and flop onto my stomach.

"You stink," Chase says.

"Thanks for saving our lives, is what this inconsiderate fellow means," Devlyn adds, nudging Chase. I sit up and wipe blue blood off my face. It's inky, which makes it sink into my clothes. It's the same color as the dragon I had faced all those months ago.

"Let's get going." I settle myself and push us out of the alcove. The remains of the squidark float around us.

CHAPTER 33

SHADOW ISLAND

The needle on the compass lights up and starts beeping frantically, waking Chase and Devlyn up. The water had gotten progressively warmer and darker, making the bubble almost cozy. It was hard not to drift off to sleep.

The sea floor starts rising as we come ashore. I launch us out of the water. Our landing isn't as smooth as I would have liked it to be.

We tumble across the sand and screech to a stop in a tangle of limbs. I groan and we manage to sit up, even though all I want to do is lie down and never get up again.

Slowly and reluctantly, we stand up and brush off the coarse sand that now coats our clothes.

"We made it," Chase says with a grin, his smile glints in the dark.

"Thank the light." I dust the remainder of sand off my black sleeves. "Let's find a place to camp for the night. We'll be able to think straighter tomorrow morning." I start digging around in my backpack for a jacket.

The cold air chills me to the bone. I find a black army jacket and zip it up. Forming a fist, a beam of light explodes from my palm when I release it, floating in the air where I command it. The beam of light grows into a mini sun, lighting up the cold beach.

We are standing on a dark beach that stretches for as far as I can see on either side of me. In front of me is a forest, well, what used to be forest. Now it is just dead limbs draped in brown moss. At our backs is the ocean from which we came. The sand is coarse, made from jagged rocks.

"Well, this place is welcoming," Chase grumbles.

Devlyn chuckles. "I couldn't agree more."

"Into the woods," I announce, tapping my necklace twice.

"Can we please not go into the Haunted Forest of Doom?" Chase asks. The temptation to throw him into the ocean is intense.

"It's the only place that is not out in the open, but if you want to be captured and die, I may let you remain in captivity," I say and walk towards the forest, Devlyn following behind me. Chase lets out an exasperated sigh and hikes after us.

The forest is even scarier from the inside. The trees pose as monsters, eerie noises echo through the hollow trees. The boughs creak as if talking about the trespassers. Darker shadows lie on the ground, making the ground feel tippy. The trees' silhouettes stand grey against the sky.

I grip the hilt of one of my blades, transferring my fear into it. I've never been good with the dark. Chase and Devlyn don't seem to mind. They go on and on about the human world.

Devlyn is fascinated by all of it. The rules, the clothes, the school system. I don't get it, the human world was so bland. I get irritated after a half hour of talking about robots. Rolia is still in my heart, which means it still hurts when robots are brought up. I think of her memory chip, tucked safely under my pillow at Hearthstone.

"Boys, let's bed down for the night," I say, my voice a hushed whisper.

We walk into a clearing the size of a truck. We set up camp, but don't light a fire. We eat a snack of ham and cheese sandwiches, still cold. Apparently, Flectes have a cellophane wrap that can keep things cold or hot for the rest of eternity. I deem it The Eternal Wrapping, which Chase says is fitting. Devlyn just rolls his eyes.

"I can take the first watch," Devlyn volunteers as we lay out our sleeping bags. "You look pretty ill, El. I think you need all the sleep you can get."

"I agree, I'll take the second watch," Chase says.

I smile. "Thanks, I think I swallowed some squid blood. And it does not sit well."

Devlyn scrunches his nose and Chase says, "Alright, that settles it. Waterbug is officially delusional."

I wish them both good night and settle into my sleeping bag, hoping I don't get eaten. And praying that the nightmares don't come too quickly.

CHAPTER 34

A SNAKE KNOCKER

I am shaken awake by a hand on my shoulder.

"We need to go," Devlyn says gruffly.

I blink the sleep out of my eyes, the cold air hitting my skin. Nothing is said as we eat our breakfast. I stuff my bedroll into my backpack and braid my knotted hair.

"Are we ready to do this?" I ask. Chase and Devlyn nod solemnly, coming to terms with where we are.

The boys and I head off, trekking west. Marching through the woods is fun, but not when you have a heavy pack, grumbly hiking mates, and a rumbling stomach. I would kill for a lemon burst right about now.

"Is that smoke?" Chase asks, pointing to something in the distance. Sure enough, a waft of smoke is floating up into the air, looking very inviting. The smell of baked goods and coffee beans wafts under my nose.

"Maybe they have food," I say weakly.

Devlyn sighs.

"Are you hearing yourselves? We're on the *Shadow Flectes'* island. People aren't nice here!"

"Maybe it's an old grandma... with cake!" Chase says, and I crack a grin.

"Cake sounds good."

"Oh, light. You two are delusional." Devlyn runs a hand down his face. "But fine! I'm bored, anyways."

"Yay!" Chase and I exclaim together.

"This is a horrible decision, really," Devlyn complains. Chase and I set out at a much faster pace.

"Oh, lighten up, Devvy," Chase says.

"Don't call me Devvy. And when you almost die, remember the wise words of Devlyn Warden."

I hardly hear them, food is calling my name. We enter a clearing and find a small cabin. Green roses grow everywhere we look.

"I'm staying back here," Devlyn says and runs back to the tree line.

Chase and I exchange glances and shrug. We walk forward and come to the door. Chase uses the knocker that is in the form of a snake to knock three times. Almost immediately an old lady opens the door.

"Ah, weary darlings! You're just in time for cake!" Chase and I exchange glances, but the smell drifting through the air is enchanting.

Chase and I are seated by the elderly woman. She smells sickly sweet, I notice. Her floral dress is strange compared to most Flectes I have seen. She has grey hair and venomous green eyes. Her pupils are small slits, like a snake's.

"Thank you so much for taking us in, ma'am. We were getting very tired and hungry," Chase says smiling.

His eyes are slightly clouded over, which isn't right. But who cares? She has food.

"Oh, of course, deariesss." She holds out her "S" like a snake.

Nothing is wrong.

"When we saw the smoke from your house, we knew happiness was close!" I say, grinning stupidly.

"Oh, many travelersss have the same experience." She smiles, and a forked tongue slithers out.

Nothing is weird about that.

"My cake is very famousss around here."

"Thank you," I say again.

She nods, smiling her oily smile. Fangs hang over her lips.

Nothing is wrong.

"I'll have that cake right out for you deariesss," she says and bows her head. Chase and I grin stupidly. The old lady leaves the room, going through a door in the back.

"It's so nice of her to take us in like this," Chase says, his smile plastered on his face.

"It is!" I respond, tapping my hand on the wooden table.

I scan my surroundings. There is a fireplace with a green plant burning in a kettle. It fills the room with green smoke. A very long snake skin hangs from the mantle.

No reason to worry.

The old lady comes back in, her smile still plastered on her scaly face. Two plates of green cake are held in her hands. She sets them before Chase and I with a smile.

"Eat up dearies. Mother S makes exceptional cake."

We pick up our forks and grin at her. I stab at the cake, raise it to my lips, and lay it on my tongue. This cake is exceptional. I've never had anything better in my life.

But something was off. My eyes focus and unfocus. The cabin begins to tip. Mother S begins to lengthen into a… SNAKE? I jump to my feet but I do it too quickly and almost fall over. Green clouds my vision. My heads pounds.

Everything is wrong. My head is clouded. I reach to double tap my necklace but my hand never makes it there, it weighs tons. The world tips upside down and I crash to the floor. I really should have heeded Devlyn Warden's words of wisdom.

CHAPTER 35

WE'VE LOST OUR MINDS

Wind, a cool breeze. Crashes, hisses, a scream of pain. Then… silence. Footsteps. Pressure on my neck and wrist.

"Oh, light. You're not dead."

A voice. A light breeze brushing my face. Arms under my back and legs. Lifting, weightlessness. Cool grass. Cold darkness.

~

My head feels like an anvil is attached to it. My eyes are glued shut with the weight of pain. I flex my fist, then bend my arm, slowly making my body work again.

With much difficulty, I sit up. Devlyn sits by a fire, cooking something. He appears to be muttering to himself.

"Have you lost your bloody head?" I ask.

Devlyn's head whips up. He stops talking to himself. Jumping to his feet he runs over to me and scoops me into his arms, holding my head against his chest. His pounding heart beat fills my ears.

"Whoa, buddy. Personal space," I croak.

But I don't push him away. I'm too weak.

"I thought you were dead, El. I was going to have to revive you!" His hands are shaking. "That snake poisoned you!"

"That's good," I say, my voice sounding like it's being rubbed against sandpaper.

"Chase?"

Devlyn nods over to a sleeping form. "I barely got you two out of there."

"He's alive?"

"Yes, now that you're awake you can do some sort of water trick to get the poison out of him." He pauses. "Right?"

"I'll try." I crawl over to Chase's sleeping form. "Hang in there, Chase."

Honestly, I have no idea what to do, but Pundit Alora had just told me to go with my gut. The water will tell me what to do. Rolling him over onto his back, I stare into his face for a moment. So peaceful, so….

I shake my head, placing my fingers on his temples. But before I can do anything, Chase coughs and I turn his head away just as he empties his stomach into the dead grass.

"Oh, gross," I say and drag Chase away from the mess. Devlyn helps me lean him against a tree and we offer him water. He takes it without saying anything and empties the entire container.

He wipes his mouth and sighs, leaning his head against the tree."You're looking awfully green there, Waterbug."

I shake my head and laugh. "You have no idea."

I stand up and wash Chase and I off with water I summon from the air. Then I instantly dry us off.

"We really need to get going. We lost two days while you were sleeping," Devlyn says, picking at the grass and tearing it up.

"Two days?" Chase and I exclaim together.

I run a hand down my face.

"That was probably the most brainless thing I have ever done. I even knew it was wrong, but I kept going. Everything was so hazy." Chase shakes his head, like he's trying to clear the fog.

"I did it too. She was a snake. She tricked us," I mutter, rubbing my forehead. "I'm pretty sure she hypnotized us."

"She definitely did. When I finally decided to go in and see if you guys were okay," Devlyn pauses, stormy eyes downcast.

"Thank you, Devvy, it means a lot."

I nod.

Devlyn sighs and continues, "She was poised over Chase with her mouth wide open."

"So, I was about to be a snake snack?" Chase asks with a shudder.

Devlyn nods, looking grim.

"It was the plant that she was burning," I say. "And when Dev came in, I felt a breeze! You must have blown it away so she couldn't have you under her spell. That was absolutely brilliant!"

"Thanks. But I don't think I was under the spell in the first place. Wind constantly swirls around me, so it couldn't sink in." Devlyn's cheeks are dotted with color.

"But seriously we need to go. Our world is probably already spiraling into chaos without the stone."

Chase and I nod slowly.

"I do have a question. Was she a Flecte? Because I thought we weren't supposed to...get old."

"No, our world is split. The dark world creates dark creatures and the light world creates light animals. She was a creature of the Dark. There's always balance to everything. That's why there are Shadow and Light Flectes. They create balance."

Chase and I stare at Devlyn. This world is a lot more complicated than I ever thought. Everything is woven together in an intricate web. And we are a part of the puzzle, and currently I am the reason it is spiraling out of control. And now I have to fix it.

I bend over and grab my bag. "Off we go. Let's hope we don't encounter any more dark creatures."

It is hard to keep walking. My head is still fuzzy. My ears ring from time to time. I have to grab a walking stick because I keep tripping over everything that my feet come in contact with.

But we keep going, knowing that we have lost so much time. The woods seem to stretch on forever. Sometimes we think that it's ending and we see the horizon, only to find that we're not even close to the end.

"If we come to another fake end of this forest, I'm going to jump from a tree," Chase mutters from behind me.

"Come on, Snake Breath, we got this."

I loop my hand through his elbow, and tug him forward. By dinner we are still in the woods, and so we bed down in yet another clearing.

"I'm going to change this forest's name from Forest of Doom, to Forest that Sucks and Goes on Forever," Chase grumbles.

Devlyn chuckles as he digs through his pack.

Untangling my hair, I manage to re-braid it. I lean against a tree, muffin in one hand and the flask that never runs dry in the other.

"Let me fly up above the treeline, and see if I can find where this forest ends," Devlyn says suddenly.

"You can fly?" I ask, my jaw hanging open.

"Yeah, if I can control the winds, I should be able to fly," he states and shoots into the air.

"Whelp, I'll add that to his list of awesomeness," Chase says and sits down on his makeshift bed.

"Oh, stop whining." I plop down on my bed across from him. "You're fine, too."

"Am I now?" He grins so wide two dimples appear at the corners of his face.

"Yes." I twist my fingers, guilt weighing on my chest. "I feel like a huge loser for going into that shed with Mother S. Everything felt wrong, and I still went in. And I led you in, as well. I'm sorry."

His sea-blue eyes twinkle. "Oh, light, be quiet! I wanted cake as much as you did. Now quit the pity party, you're making me sick."

"Fine," I say reluctantly, even though I'm grinning.

He shakes his head and starts eating his sandwich. Devlyn chooses that exact moment to touch down beside him. Like he was waiting for our conversation to be over.

"It looks like we have another twenty miles in that direction." He points toward the east, the opposite direction of the setting sun.

"Twenty miles, that'll be two more days in this never-ending forest of doom!" Chase grumbles, voicing my own thoughts.

"Yup," Devlyn says and sits on his own sleeping bag. The boys eat their dinner in silence, lost in their thoughts.

"I'll take the first watch tonight," I offer.

Devlyn probably has not slept in two days. He deserves the rest. Chase shoots me a look as if he knows I'm tired, but he doesn't object. Chase deserves sleep too. He almost got eaten.

They fall asleep instantly. Their gentle snores are oddly comforting. But it still leaves me alone in the Forest of Doom. I pull out one of my longer throwing knives, making me feel a little better.

I sit and whittle a stick into a spear with intricate designs on the side. It helps me pass the hours till the moon is directly above us, signaling that it is midnight. Which means it's Chase's shift. Feeling bad, I shake him awake. He sits up looking startled.

"It's okay, it's just your shift." I say in the same voice I use to calm Bliss.

"Oh, okay. Sorry, I was dreaming about snakes," he admits and pulls himself off his bed and onto a log two feet from my sleeping bag. I climb in and my muscles relax as the warmth settles into my skin.

CHAPTER 36

THE DREAM AND THE KISS

"Muriel Wiley, how nice of you to join me here." A hand covered in scars reaches out and brushes a strand of hair back from my forehead.

I jump back but find I am standing on the edge of a cliff. Dark waves crash below me.

"Who are you?" I scream into the dark. A faceless figure steps forward.

"The King of the Dark, your worst nightmare, Killer of Kings." The faceless figure pauses. A cowl hides his face and body. But he appears faceless. "I have many names. We shall meet soon enough again. My minions are awakening. You have met some of them. They have told me you have your strengths and weaknesses. Just as everyone, of course."

"You'll never hurt me!" I scream, my heels are on the edge of the cliff now.

"I already have." There is a smile in his voice. "We shall meet again soon, my young queen." And with that, the scarred hands reach forward and shove me off the cliff.

I sit bolt upright, a scream on my lips but unable to escape. Sweat trickles down my temples. I glance at Chase and he is staring at the rising sun, unharmed.

"Ch-Chase," I say, fear laced in my stomach. He whips his head toward me, his eyes going wide when he sees the terror in my face.

"The King of Darkness visited me." He kneels beside me and brushes a sweaty strand of hair out of my eyes. I shudder, remembering the scarred hand doing the same thing.

"El...." His eyebrows are etched together. Worry in his voice and his eyes.

I shake my head. "He spoke to me in a dream and pushed me off a cliff. He called me a queen..." I finger my necklace. "I think...I think he killed our parents."

Chase stares at me for a moment. "Muriel, I think you're really shaken up. That poison. It must be doing things to your head. Everything's going to be okay. Just trust."

"Just trust?" I ask, skeptical.

Chase grins, but not enough to show his secret dimples. "Yeah, just trust the process. Trust that we'll get through this."

"Okay," I say with a nod, but my hands don't stop shaking.

"Good, now let's wake Dev, he looks too happy sleeping."

The dream stays with me. As we hike, my thoughts keep circling back to the scarred hands, pushing me off the cliff. And his words, "Killer of Kings." Fear makes my knees shake at times, but I don't show Devlyn and Chase.

I have to be strong for them. Just as they have been strong for me.

My pack begins to weigh me down around dusk. And Devlyn notices. We decide to set up camp. We eat our dinner, the same food we've had the last couple days. It's getting annoyingly repetitive.

Devlyn checks our distance. By his estimation we have another ten miles just like he said. Devlyn takes the first watch, so Chase and I crash into a heavy sleep. But dreams won't stay away from me.

~

"El." The word is spoken softly.

"Not again," I whisper, spinning in the dark. I can see nothing, feel nothing. My fingers brush against cold air when I extend them, searching for answers.

"Do not be afraid."

"I'm in the dark, a weird voice is speaking to me, and I got shoved off a cliff last night. So yes, I'm allowed to be afraid."

A gentle laugh. A shining light.

I hold my hands up, blocking the bright light. Its radiance is almost too much.

"Your dreams are increasing as you near the home of the Dark. And so, I have brought something to protect you."

"Who are you?"

"Your past, your present, and your future."

"Oh joy, more elusive names."

A gentle finger presses against my lips. "Do not be afraid."

It was a command this time, so I remain silent.

"I have a gift for you. Protection. Its magic will wear off in a month's time but you will always have its sign." A woman dressed in white steps forward. Her smile is brilliant.

"Do not be afraid, Muriel Wiley." She places a kiss on my cheek then disappears. I cry out in pain as my cheek burns. Then the pain disappears. And I am left alone.

My eyes pop open. I feel for my cheek. No pain. Nothing.

I sit up and glance around. Chase and Devlyn sit by the fire, talking and smiling. I sigh and shove my sleeping bag off.

I plop down next to them. "Morning," I say.

"Mor—whoa, El. Something's on your cheek," Chase says, eyes wide. Devlyn looks afraid.

"It's the sign of the Estrella," he murmurs.

"Who, now?" I ask, glancing at Chase.

He shakes his head, sharing my confusion.

"The kings and queens of old. The sun came down and blessed them with special powers. Or at least that's what my Zilliad History teacher told me."

"I got kissed by a queen," I say, touching my cheek.

Chase laughs. "It looks kind of cool, honestly. It's a sun–star thing."

"Ugh, how big is it?" I sigh. "She said it will last forever."

Devlyn makes a thinking noise then walks away, beginning to pack his stuff.

"Oh, about the size of a penny." Chase cocks his head. "It's golden too, which is crazy. I can't believe you have two tattoos by the age of fifteen."

"Great," I say.

We eat a quick breakfast of still-warm muffins and pack up our stuff. Forest life is returning…somewhat. There are small animals now singing in the still-dead boughs. The moss has gone from brown to murky green.

My legs are aching and my pants are in tatters from the thorns that line our path. We have to go over a small mountain. It is covered in bristly bushes. I would choose to be anywhere else than here right now.

During a break, we sit cross legged, eating our lunch, when we hear the first howl. My head whips up. I double tap my necklace, instinct acting for me.

"This is going to be fun," Devlyn grunts, jumping to his feet. He grabs his spear from behind his back. I hear Chase's sword unsheathe.

Another howl goes up from the woods, louder this time. I let out a little whimper as the first wolf appears. It is twice the size of a normal wolf, and has red glowing eyes. Muscles ripple under its black coat, teeth dripping with saliva and red stuff. That, I don't want to know any more about.

It's joined by three others, looking equally as hungry, and equally as ferocious. I grab a long dagger from my vest, ready to fight to the death. Apparently, Chase is the only one with a working head because he shouts, "CLIMB!" and races to the nearest tree. The Wolfzillas are momentarily surprised by our sudden movement. I sprint to a tree, and scramble up the dead branches, begging them to not break. I pray that I am far enough away from the Wolfzilla who is clawing at the tree. Its claws tear at the wood. I scan the trees for Chase and Devlyn. Chase is three trees away to my right with his sword drawn, and Devlyn is one tree away on Chase's right.

"What are we going to do?" I yell at them from my tree, gripping my knife.

"Destroy them? I mean there's only four—" Another wolf jumps into the clearing cutting Chase off. "Oh—" he finishes with a sigh of disgust, "—I hate this place so much."

"Same, let's destroy them." Devlyn says and lets his spear fly at the first wolf. It hits one perfectly in the throat. It falls over with a sickening sound. I clench my teeth. It isn't time to be squeamish.

"Okay, so they can die. That's a good thing, but what am I supposed to do, sit up here while you guys destroy?" Chase asks, frowning and holding up his sword.

"Unless you want to go down there and hack away?" I challenge and throw a knife at the nearest wolf. I hit it in the eye, and it collapses. Two are left. But then more howls go up and five more race into the clearing. Our odds are not looking great for survival.

"I'm good!" Chase yells from his tree.

I throw knife after knife. Devlyn summons his spear and throws it again and again. But no matter how many we cut down the wolves just keep coming. My arm begins to feel heavy.

"What if we are in their territory? I bet if we leave it, they won't bother us," I speculate.

I have no other options. Things are looking bad for us.

"Okay, good plan. Now how do we get down without getting mauled?" Chase asks me.

"Good question," I say and think out loud, "We need a distraction."

Chase and Devlyn look skeptical, but I just concentrate. I call water from deep inside the ground, pulling enough together for a tidal wave. I push it out of the ground, washing a couple wolves away. A tidal wave should have done more damage.

"Get out of the trees! I'll wash us away!"

I quickly form it into a wall as we scramble down. A branch breaks and I fall the last ten feet and lose concentration. I hit the ground and the air gets knocked out of my chest. I hear my name screamed.

I glance up and find the wall of water collapsing and washing towards us in a giant wave at least twenty feet high. I didn't think I had summoned that much. Someone yells a battle cry as it bears down on us. Attempting to stand up, I find that my legs no longer work. I am too fatigued after calling all of that water. With the last of my energy I wrap a protective bubble around Chase and Devlyn, letting the water crash down on us.

The water hits me with so much force it takes my breath away for the second time today.

The water swirls and whirls as if it has a mind of its own. It finds a ravine and washes down it, knocking trees down. They crash into the water around us. I catch sight of Chase clinging to a log. I pull him back under the water with the current and wrap him in a bubble. I do the same for Devlyn. Even though I can't find him, I can still feel him through the water.

I squeeze my eyes shut, concentrating on not letting Chase and Devlyn drown. My breaths come short under the water as it churns around me. My face gets scraped by branches, but I hold onto the connection. I can feel their panic through the water, and I apologize silently. I brought this down upon us. A huge log bears down on me and I hardly have the strength to lift my arm. Suddenly a bright flash appears and the log turns to ash. My cheek sears.

Protection. I'm being protected. I guess I'm not the only Protector.

When I feel like I can't hold the boys up any longer, I see the end. The ravine spills out onto a prairie. The water disperses into the dead grass, and I release the boys.

I don't even have the strength to sit up. The water pools around my face. Water is in my eyes, ears, and nose. I cough.

"Oh, light! Is she dead?" Splashing.

"El!" My face is turned towards Chase and Devlyn with gentle warm fingers. I manage a smile.

"How are you smiling! We almost drowned!" Chase is looking panicked. Devlyn is trying to find if I'm injured at all.

"I'm fine, Dev." I take a deep breath. "Just tired is all."

"Remind me to never listen to a Water Flecte when she says she has a way out." Chase says, smiling at me. But he has tears in his eyes. "But thanks for saving us, anyways."

"I…didn't let you drown, genius," I say, hacking up water.

"You got rid of the wolves," Chase says smiling.

"I did indeed." Devlyn leans back, grey eyes stormy.

I can never tell if he is angry or just content with an evil look.

"We need to find a place to camp. Chase, do you mind carrying her? I'll get the packs." Chase nods and lifts me into his arms. If I wasn't so tired, I would be embarrassed.

Chase carries me while following Devlyn. I feel my eyes being weighed down by exhaustion. They slowly slide shut. The last thing they see are dark spires reaching towards the sky set by an orange sun.

CHAPTER 37

THE BLACK SPIRES

Devlyn shakes my shoulder waking me up. It's morning. My entire body is sore, like I had just done the hardest workout of a lifetime.

"Here, drink this." Devlyn hands me a cup. It has dried up leaves in it.

I eye him, then take a sip. Instantly, I feel better. Warmth courses through my bones, washing away the pain. I gulp it down. My muscles are no longer aching.

"Wow, this stuff is amazing. What is it?" I hand the cup back to him. Remembering the drink Ash gave to me during my second day of school and Ravenscroft makes my heart ache. I miss her.

"Terra Leaf, a Flecte special." He cracks a dazzling smile, and stands up. "My mother gave me the herbal mixture to make it, thinking we may need some "medicinals" and now I'm glad I brought it."

"Me too," I croak, lying my head back on the ground.

I survey where we are camped out. The stone walls of the cave have small trails of water running down them. Stalagmites and stalactites reaching to meet each other. A trickling stream runs through the center, slightly murky. Minute birds scuttle along the walls, their luminescent bodies blinking.

I climb out of the sleeping bag. Chase sits, his back against the one dry wall, wrapping his sword hilt in black leather. Walking over, I plop myself down next to him, taking out my knives. I clean off the wolf blood.

"Today's the day," he says, his voice quiet.

"Yeah." I wipe the blade I am holding clean. "I guess it is."

Shifting in the sand, I turn and find Chase's eyes on me. "Whatever happens, El, promise me you won't forget me." His words take me aback.

I stutter, trying to find words. "Chase…." My voice catches in my throat. "Nothing is going to happen."

"No, of course not. Just promise me, please?"

"Okay, I promise."

~

Black spires reach towards the smog-filled sky. The ground is muddy, even though it hasn't been walked on in ages. The air is putrid, and my lungs scream for fresh air, but I have nothing to relieve them with. Prairies of dead grass stretch around us. It appears to have burned, and then someone decided they liked it, and they liked it enough to build a scary castle right in the middle of it.

We're still a couple miles away from the castle, but we're too close for my liking. If we fail, the whole world falls apart. It's all on us now.

The stress riding on my shoulders is like nothing I have ever felt before. I feel myself stop breathing at times when I realize what we are heading into. But it's what we were born to do, we've been training for this. Every moment of my life the last several months seems to be leading up to this moment. And I won't back down, even though I want to.

We don black hooded cloaks, which help us blend into the dark landscape. I don't see the point. No one is expecting us to come. Who would be crazy enough to threaten the Shadow Flectes? And infiltrate their island?

At dusk we reach the outskirts of a black city. Huge black walls tower above us. We had already agreed to storm the castle during the cover of night. But this city is already black during the day. My stomach twists into knots.

"I can fly one of you over at a time," Devlyn offers. I wrap my arms around his neck, and he carries me over in a gust of light air.

"Thanks," I say with a smile as he touches down lightly.

"Anytime." He stares at me for a second too long and my cheeks warm.

"Hellooooo?" Chase's voice comes over the wall. "I'm left alone in the dark on the outskirts of the City of Doom. Please come get me, Superman."

Devlyn rolls his eyes and shoots over the wall, reappearing with Chase in his arms. I laugh at the sight of them. They touch down, and Chase pats Devlyn's shoulder with a grin. Devlyn just glares at the ground.

We scan our surroundings. The town is made out of black marble. Black streets, black houses, black torches filled with red fire.

We creep through the quiet streets. There must be a curfew, because the streets are dead. No one seems to be around. All of the shadows stand still. Just breathing feels too loud. Shapes appear like monsters on the walls.

My palms are sweating so ferociously I drop the knife I'm holding. It clatters to the ground, the noise ringing off the buildings. I wince and pick it up carefully. No one moves. No one breathes.

"This is too easy," I whisper.

"I agree, they must not be expecting anyone." Devlyn holds his hand up to wait.

We are on the outskirts of the courtyard that leads to the castle. Guards line the towering gate. Cold light shines from the windows.

The forms of life relieve me. I was beginning to think everyone was gone.

We begin to go up an alley that will lead around to the back of the castle, but I am stopped by Devlyn waving his arms frantically. We screech to a stop and creep back into the shadows, holding our breath.

Approximately two hundred soldiers march around the building we are hiding behind. I close my eyes, wishing I could disappear. I hold my breath until their rhythmic footsteps fade away.

"That was too close," I say, holding my stomach.

"Way too close," Devlyn says.

Continuing on, we creep around to the back of the castle, using the back alleys, keeping to the shadows. The back gates are unguarded but are equally as tall as the ones in front. Spikes as long as my arm stick out of the top.

Fear tangles in my stomach. My breathing shortens. This is it. We've made it to the gates.

"Out of the danger zone " Chase says, a grim smirk on his lips, "And into the death zone."

CHAPTER 38

JUST TRUST, EL

"I think it's time to use the Invisibility Drink," I whisper to Devlyn. He nods and takes out three bottles of shimmery gloop. He hands one to me, then another to Chase.

I turn it over and read the instructions.

Wears off after thirty turns of full dose. You will be visible to your friends who join you in the mysterious land of invisibility. But the rest of the world will never know you were there! Swallow quickly, and enjoy!

Popping off the cork lid, I tip it back. It slides down my throat. I fight the urge to barf.

"Bleh," Chase says, from beside me, sticking his tongue out. "That wath dithguthting."

"Do you think it worked?" I ask. Chase shrugs and looks at the guards that stand in the courtyard.

"Yo, my boys! What's up?" Chase shouts.

I turn on him, shocked. Then I realize he's shimmering, like his entire body got attacked by a fairy. That must show the invisibility.

Yet the guards remain expressionless.

"Guess so," Devlyn says and pushes through the towering gate and across the marble courtyard. A tall wooden doorway is the only thing that stands between us and the Hope Stone now. Besides whoever lives in the castle, of course.

Chase walks through one of the guards. He does an evil laugh that only we can hear. I cannot help but laugh also. We walk through the front door, and enter the Pit of Darkness.

~

Black walls with silver chandeliers hang from the ceiling, casting eerie shadows upon us. There are statues of wolves and dragons standing along the walls. Their opal eyes seem to follow us. I have to remind myself that I am invisible.

The halls are empty—too empty. I am so accustomed to my white halls and crystal chandeliers. Everything around us feels so dark, and heavy.

We creep along, and pass door after door. Blaze told us that the king probably has the Hope Stone in his throne room out for display, as if tempting someone to come and get it. Blaze also told us that the royal family was extremely arrogant.

That explains keeping their prizes out on display. It also explains all of the portraits of a blonde man smiling creepily, hanging on the walls. We finally come to an ornate door with runes above it that none of us can read.

"You think this is the one?" I ask, my voice in a hushed whisper.

Devlyn points to the rune in the center. A hooded figure in a crown. "That's the sign for royalty. So, probably."

"Ladies and gents, I present you the throne room of the King of Shadow Island." And with that, Chase pushes through the tall door. And all I can do is follow him.

The first thing I notice is the magnificence of the room we enter. A huge circular cathedral with a domed ceiling, and three thrones standing in front of a huge tapestry of a star being swallowed by a shadow.

On the throne in the center is a man with a black crown and blonde hair. He looks frustrated. He's the man from the portraits that were hanging on the walls.

On the right of him is a boy about our age with blonde hair, and disturbing sky-blue eyes. They are rimmed with gold, and so blue, they look like jewels set into his head, but they look haunted. And on the king's right is... is... the girl who stole the stone. I grip Devlyn's arm and point to the girl.

"Can you just hand me the throne, already?" The girl asks, twisting her stunning blonde hair. "I stole the stone, I deserve it. Flint failed twice to serve you."

The king shakes his head. "Ivy, how many times have I told you that you are to split the kingdom?" The girl rolls her eyes at the king. "You and Flint both have your strengths. And weaknesses."

He looks pointedly at his son. The young prince sighs and slouches in his throne.

Happy family.

The king pulls out a glowing green jewel that makes my fingers itch.

The Hope Stone.

I feel captivated by its warmth and light. I want to move but am unable. Devlyn chooses that moment to take action, right when I'm not able to move.

With a blast of wind, he knocks the jewel out of the king's hand. His sudden movement brings me back to reality. I run and grab it, putting it into my pants pocket. Its warmth radiates through me and I feel instantly full of hope.

But there is another problem. Its power seems to be wearing off my invisibility. And it's not doing it slowly.

My whole arm is already in plain sight, having lost its shimmery appearance. I make a mad dash for the door, noticing that both Chase and Devlyn are gone. Maybe now that I am becoming visible I can no longer see them. I pray that they are still near me.

"What is this?" The king asks as he looks around.

I reach the door just as I become fully visible. The king and his children gasp. Ivy snarls, which is something I don't want to see ever again.

The boy gets over his shock first and summons a ball of fire, launching it at me. I have never fought fire before so it surprises me a little bit. Good thing I have water.

I dive to the ground, the fire ball smashing just above my head on the wall. I get to my knees and put my hands on the floor, closing my eyes and breathing deeply. I summon the water from below the castle. There must be a whole lake down there because the force I feel coming is not something to be messed with. My whole body tingles as the floor shakes.

Portraits crash to the ground. The floor explodes as a tidal wave appears and crashes towards them. The boy dives out of the way of the wave and screams in rage. His sister and father disappear from the force of water.

The wave hits the wall and begins to come after me. I catch the hatred in the boy's gleaming eyes as we both run out doors that lead off the throne room.

I run through the halls at a sprint, hoping the boys are safe, but feeling angry that they abandoned me. Adrenaline courses through my veins as I crash through the halls, knocking over tables. I run as fast as my long legs will carry me.

Fear is pulsing through my limbs, urging me to go faster. I feel a presence gaining on me. I get tackled to the ground.

I yell in rage and try to get up, but I am pinned. I turn my face and find the Prince of the Shadow Flectes. His blonde hair covering his eyes.

"You thought you could get away, didn't you?" he asks and tilts his head.

His eyes reflect the fire he holds inside him. I shudder. He tries to punch me, but I move my head to the side quickly. He growls in frustration.

"CHASE!" I scream at the top of my lungs.

Not exactly heroic, but I am beginning to feel exhausted. Summoning tidal waves isn't exactly easy on the body.

Chase appears above me with his classic smirk.

He punches Flint in the face so hard, I hear a crack. I flinch a little. Flint moans and topples off of me. Chase pulls me to my feet and grabs my hand sprinting towards the door.

"Come on, El, just a little further. You can do it." He drags me along, but my legs feel like jelly. The back doors stand open. The dark courtyard is alight with torches. One hundred guards stand, rage and hatred in all of their eyes. Some hold fire in their hands, ready for attack.

"You will kindly lower your weapons and return the Hope Stone." Their voices are synchronized.

Now this. This is the end. There is no way out. No more tricks to pull out of our sleeves. No more tidal wave escapes or winds to sweep us away.

"Good bye, Chase," I say, closing my eyes.

"You will drop your weapons, and listen to me." An eerie voice. Too high pitched and too low. I spin to find its source.

The guards all drop their weapons and bow their heads. My head whips up to Chase. The voice is coming from him. His eyes are glowing.

Mind control, I realize, but it is too late.

"Muriel, leave now with Devlyn, I will see you in a little bit."

Chase releases my hand. Devlyn lands beside me in a swirl of wind. His eyes are clouded over. He's almost unrecognizable. My mind is numb, every instinct telling me to stay, to help him.

There is no compulsion telling me to not listen to his voice. It's just me and the voice telling me what to do. Chase is totally and completely in control of me.

"Okay," I say numbly, not knowing why I am listening. But I have the urge to do whatever he tells me to do. My arms and legs aren't my own. My head isn't my own. I would jump off a cliff for him.

He bends down, and kisses my forehead. "Just trust, El."

I stand there, eyes blank. A pair of arms wrap around my waist, blasting us out of the city. Devlyn looks disturbed as we fly over the land that we had hiked. My mind feels foggy, like I'm lost in a dream.

"What's wrong?" I ask.

"I don't know, but something doesn't feel right." Devlyn plunges us into the ocean and my mind comes back to me. Guilt crashes into me like a tidal wave.

"We left him behind! How could we do that? How could you let this happen?" Bubbles come out of my mouth as I rise towards the surface. I shake Devlyn, grabbing his shoulders, trying to get him out of whatever trance he is in.

His eyes remain unfocused. He yanks the necklace from my neck and pulls off the compass. He opens it up, tapping it twice. A bubble, not formed by me, comes out of the compass and shoots us forward. Wind binds me, I am unable to fight, unable to change the currents to take me back.

It was supposed to be me. If anyone was going to be left behind, it should have been me. All of this was my fault. A soft voice enters my mind.

Just trust. The voice is weak. I shake my head, unable to move. Sobs rack my body. The force shoots us out of the water and onto the wharf of Coastina.

The clouds in Devlyn's eyes clear. My bonds of air fall away. He collapses onto the pier, head in his hands. We hold each other as we cry, unable to get up. Unable to move.

We left him.

He made you.

We left him.

The voices in my mind rage. Scarred hands and the shadowy voice fill my head again. The Queen's Kiss can't protect me from this darkness.

A voice calls in the distance, "They're back!"

I hear footsteps heading towards us. I do not have the heart to look. Do not have the energy. Warm arms pick me up, and someone pours a liquid down my throat. I nod off into a land of sea-blue eyes and scarred hands.

CHAPTER 39

HELLO, MURIEL

The world is upside down. Pain courses through my body. I ache. Everywhere.

I thrash and scream. Calling for the one I left behind. The dreams are the worst though. They torture me.

Plunging me in and out of the darkness. The pain in me eats away at the Queen's Kiss and the protection it brought. Until a sliver of darkness pours even more shadows into my head.

The laugh. The one I never wanted to return. And scarred hands, reaching for my throat.

"Hello, Muriel."

ACKNOWLEDGEMENTS

My dear readers, I am so grateful for you. You are what made this whole dream of mine possible. You are the ones who bring this story to life. Without you this story would just be pages inside a spine. So thank you, for joining me in this story, in this adventure.

First, I want to thank God for giving me the gift to be able to write stories. You are the true story teller, and the truest hero. I have a lot to learn from you.

Secondly, I would like to thank you, Gram, for being my right hand woman in this journey. And for editing and puzzling over every sentence with me over quarantine. Our little chat times really did help carry me through! You are the most faithful partner that I have had during the last three years. I'm guessing you've read this story more times than I have! Basically, I totally adore and love you! I couldn't have done this without you.

Audrey, Lucy, you my darlings are who helped me rethink this entire story and name these characters. And for fangirling with me over my own characters. You two gave me reason to continue writing. Audrey, thank you for the honesty and tips that you gave me and for staying up late to read with me at our sleepovers. (And I might still take you up on that one plot tip you gave me, *if* you keep it a secret) Lucy, you also have read this story more times than I have, and your begging for more chapters is a reason there is a book two and three.

Asher Johnson, thank you for your witty remarks and points and CRAZY plot twists that you give me (they really make me rethink my entire story). You help me stay in the realm of being real, and that is something that I am eternally grateful for.

Mom and Dad, I understand how hard it is having a writer for a daughter. That week of Thanksgiving when Genius was Burning and I couldn't stop writing. Thank you for loving and supporting me through this. I owe these words to you, Mom, you did teach me how to read and write afterall. And Dad, for giving me the sense of adventure and telling me stories and reading the entire Lord of the Rings series to me as a seven year old. You both instilled in me this sense of creativity, and for that I am forever indebted to you.

Peyton Williamson, my trusted adviser, my closest friend, my business assistant. Thank you for helping me stay organized and talking to me for hours. And for being my best friend. I love you!

And Gabi Lind, for being the first person I ever showed this story to and for helping me develop a love for writing. 8th Grade Creative Writing class with you taught me so much! (you taught me more than our teacher did) And for editing with me and helping me design cover #1.

ANI!!!!!! My magnificent lovely artist, *you* helped bring my characters alive! I could not be more happy every time you send me the art. I swear I dance around my house singing every time you send me the art. I am so grateful!

And thank you everyone, for listening to me when I vented about the late nights and couldn't seem to get my mind off this story. I adore all of you, my sweet friends.

For all of you who helped this dream come true, thank you. You are more precious to me than you would ever know. I adore all of you and could not be more grateful for your investment in this dream of mine.

Thank you!!

Love, Lil. :)

I have included Chapter 1 from book two. If you have not read this book stop and turn back, *spoilers ahead*!

CHAPTER 1

CHASE

I'm not dead yet. That's the only thing that's keeping me sane. I've been down in this stinky pit for a while now, and I've experienced things that I would prefer not to even think about. Every day is the same: my only meal arrives in the morning, then interrogation by Flint, the prince of the Shadow Flectes, about the girl who destroyed his throne room and stole back the Hope Stone, and I sleep with burns on my skin in the shape of his hands. I try to stay sane by moving around, but it's just a little bit difficult when you're burned, starving, and living in a dirty cell covered in grime.

Apparently Muriel drowned the king, so his son isn't the happiest person alive right now. I've gotten used to it by now, and I'm good at hiding my feelings. I mean, you kinda have to after you've lost your mom in a car accident, got magically dropped into a city of light people that tell you that your old life was fake, and watched someone that matters a lot to you get whisked away by another boy. Yes, that would be El.

Yeah. My life couldn't be better.

I'm currently devouring my only meal of the day: a stale piece of bread the size of my palm and a glass of lukewarm water. My stomach is now the size of a walnut thanks to my restricted diet. My dirt covered clothes hang loosely on my frail frame and paper-thin skin sticks to my ribs. Holes are scattered all over from Flint's form of saying hello. I've never actually thought about how I'd always had the right amount of food to satisfy me until now. It makes me take a step back and rethink life. It's humbling, really.

Stale hay in the corner is the only thing I have to sleep on, besides the floor. Metal lanterns adorn the walls, their light flickering across the dark walls. I stare in envy at the clean, stone ground outside my cell and the cold, nasty floor I sit on. On the walls are white tally marks that mark each day of my imprisonment. Four weeks and three days exactly.

My hygiene is driving me nuts. It isn't the fact that I'm imprisoned from my family and friends; it's the fact that my body is slowly rotting away. I can't believe how much my stink can bother me as much as it is.

I stand up when I hear footsteps coming down the corridor. Flint and two guards appear at the door. Flint's piercing blue eyes stab mine, his olive toned skin shining in contrast to his dark clothes. His height is only to my shoulder but he has an aura of strength. Maybe it's the crown resting on his brow.

Anger fuels up inside me, but I force a smirk.

"Let's make our little chat short today. I don't like to stay away from my cage too long. It ruins my depressed, stinky human vibe," I say. Humor has always been my coverup. It removes the hurt that's constantly hanging in the background, waiting to swallow me up.

"Really, you're still full of it?" Flints asks, glaring at me. His sky blue eyes flash even colder.

"Yessir! You are trying your best, so, great job." I give him a thumbs up.

Flint's cheeks flush. "Fine. Come on. We have to talk."

"Sorry, man. These smelly bars are in my way," I remind him, patting the metal bars that are keeping me from escape. I cringe as I notice the grime caked under my nails. I force myself to stay calm even though I feel the panic rising in the back of my throat.

Flint doesn't say anything as he motions for the guards to let me out. The metal gate swings open.

As I follow Flint through the halls, the guards begin to hang back, which I find a bit odd. Without the guards at my heels, I could probably take Flint down.

And then what? There is no way out. I've thought about it often enough.

Flint leads me to a large oak door and pushes it open, revealing a plush sitting room. Scarlet recliners adorn the room, sitting atop black marble. Shadowy grey chandeliers hang from the ceiling, making it feel more ominous than comfortable. Flint motions for me to take a seat, and then he lowers himself into an overstuffed armchair across from me. I haven't been in this room yet. It's only been a dark chamber with no light.

"Bring it on," I mutter, secretly dreading his reply. I expect something like "We're going to fatten you up before we eat you muahahaha" or "Don't worry only some of us are cannibals."

But what comes out of his mouth is something that almost blows me out of my already uncomfortable seat.

"I want to hear your story."

I sit there for a moment, just staring at him. "Wait. What did you say?"

His eyes lock onto mine. "I'm being serious. I want to hear your story."

I squint at him a moment, still trying to process what he was trying to say. *First this guy wants to torture me to death, and now he's asking to hear my* story*?*

Five seconds flutter past. I frown, then shrug. What harm could it do?

"Fine. It all started with a pair of beautiful green eyes on a bus."

A Fiery Heart:

A Short Story from Flint Nighttide's Point of View

Rain crashes down on my island. My knees sink into the mud below me. I reach my hand out and touch my father's gravestone.

Why did she have to take him from me? She could've just left us alone to do what we needed to do with the Stone. All we wanted was hope for our people.

But I can't focus on that. There are more things at play. More things that are taking up the space inside my brain. I can't just wallow in my grief and anger.

I stand up and walk back towards my dark castle, my mind swirling with darkness and schemes. But I can't think of it now. I have to move on. Besides, it was not like my dad was even loving. But I'm not going to immerse you in my family drama.

Don't even get me started on my sister. She hasn't stopped bothering me about wanting to be queen. Blah blah blah. She's already the queen of drama, isn't that enough?

I open the back door of my castle and tromp inside. I pass the door to the dungeon, and my stomach twists. I'll have to hurt that Chase kid tomorrow, but in a few days' time, it'll all be over. He'll know the secret.

I enter the dining room and find my sister, Ivy, sitting at the table, pushing her food around her plate. Her blonde hair is flawless as always, and her white gown is encrusted with diamonds. I will never understand why she likes to dress up so much. I heave a sigh and go over to sit with her. Even though she is the most annoying thing that has ever happened to me, she's still my sister.

I sit down across from her and load my plate up with food that is piled on the table. Roast beef resting on a plate of squash drizzled with thyme and butter. A slice of cake rich with chocolate and layered with light whipping cream. She glances up at me and narrows her eyes.

"Hello brother," she hisses and twists her blonde intricate braid.

"Hello sister," I respond in an equally cool voice.

"How was your day?" I ask, trying to start a conversation.

"Fine, I think our tutor is getting more annoying," she mutters, taking me by surprise. She normally just says "Fine," then goes on ignoring me.

"Yeah, Madam Loola's the worst."

Ivy blinks her large blue eyes at me then goes back to her food. Back to ground zero. I know that she's my only family left (besides a very cranky grandpa that I prefer not to think about) so I try to be kind to her…most of the time.

"I think I'm going to go to bed," she mutters and slips out of the room before I can say anything else. At least we didn't argue tonight.

I finish my food in silence, not tasting the delicacies that were placed before me by my personal chef. I gotta tell you, being a prince is not all what it is summed up to be. Everyone has opinions. Everyone tells you how to rule.

Most people hate you. But I've gotten used to it by now. The Hope Stone was my only chance for my people to be happy again.

Well…there is another chance…but it probably is not going to happen anytime soon.

You have the key to it in your basement, a voice whispers to me in my head. I push the thought away. Having a

Light Flecte as an enemy and being friends with a Light Flecte are two different things. And for my plan to work, I have to be friends with one.

So, for now, I will wait, be patient until the time is right. There is no other way. Suddenly, I'm being pulled into a flashback and the table disappears.

"Flint," a soft warm voice calls to me.

I jerk around and find my mother, blonde, smiling, and beautiful. So kind. So gentle.

"Mom?" I ask and go to pinch myself. My mother died years ago.

"No! Flint! I have a message for you!" she calls and walks towards me, a shining light in my dark sleeping mind.

"Mom, I—" She steps up to me and puts a finger to my lips.

"Not now, this is important. You have to bring our worlds together again. Please, Flint. I see a light in you that your sister doesn't contain. I know that you know that it has to happen. Hate is not the answer, peace is. I have watched from the stars. Things are happening, you must bring the Day and Night together. You have to." She begins to fade away and I reach out to her.

"Don't leave me, Mom."

"I believe in you, my prince." All that is left of her is a soft and gentle breeze.

I jerk out of my flashback and glance around. That has never happened before. My mother. She had been different from the rest of us Shadow Flectes. She had been kind and gentle. She had tried to teach me to be the same, but my dad had won half of that war.

Kindness is the only way, Flint, my mom would always remind me. It is the only way. I will change this. It might take time. But I will.

For my mother. For everyone. For the girl with the green eyes, who fought so hard for her people. For the boy who sacrificed himself. And no one will change my mind.

L. D. Warken grew up in the small town of Etna, California when she discovered her love for writing. At the age of thirteen, she wrote her first story. Her love for writing grew and she furthered her adventure as a writer. Lover of cake, rainy days, and a good book, Lily pursued to give readers a sense of adventure. She wants to give her readers a story that they will enjoy just as she enjoyed the stories that she read as a little girl.

CPSIA information can be obtained
at www.ICGtesting.com
Printed in the USA
FSHW010414150321
79448FS